A Virgin on the Rocks

In 1933 Bernard Fosdyke, aspiring novelist, believing in common with others of his ilk and generation that Berlin was where the action was, squandered his patrimony in getting there and ended up on the rocks. But Berlin had just become the headquarters of a new and ugly political movement, as a result of which Bernard had to leave hastily for Paris, inseparably accompanied by an iron grating with *Berliner Stadtwerke* inscribed upon it.

Which is how he came to meet Harold Hiram Levy, art forger, late of the Bronx, and Levy —'Call me Hal'—was quick to detect a latent talent in Bernard: he had a criminal mind.

Hal did not believe in talents lying idle. Especially when he had need of them to devise a scheme whereby the Louvre's version of one of Leonardo da Vinci's masterpieces could be exchanged for his handmade copy.

For a cool half-million Bernard was ready to help—but his heart wasn't in it, being in thrall to an enchanting young woman who accepted lifts from importuning gentlemen in limousines.

Nevertheless, with the unwitting assistance of Gertrude Stein*, Ernest Hemingway, Henry Miller, Pablo Picasso and Jean Cocteau, not to mention the Temporary Acting Director of the Louvre, the night of the switch dawned. And with it, trouble . . .

*and Alice B. Toklas, of course

MICHAEL BUTTERWORTH

A Virgin
on the Rocks

Variations on a Theme in the Black Manner

COLLINS, 8 GRAFTON STREET, LONDON W1

William Collins Sons & Co. Ltd
London · Glasgow · Sydney · Auckland
Toronto · Johannesburg

First published 1985
© Michael Butterworth 1985

British Library Cataloguing in Publication Data

Butterworth, Michael
A virgin on the rocks.—(Crime Club)
I. Title
823'.914   PR6052.U9

ISBN 0 00 231420 7

Photoset in Linotron Baskerville by
Rowland Phototypesetting Ltd
Bury St Edmunds, Suffolk
Printed in Great Britain by
William Collins Sons & Co. Ltd, Glasgow

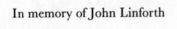
In memory of John Linforth

ON THE ROCKS. (Br. Colloq.) To be 'stony broke'. Having no financial liquidity. Bankrupt. (US colloq.) Spirituous liquor poured into a glass filled with ice cubes: e.g. 'Scotch on the rocks'.

Marlowe's Dictionary of Common English Cant Words and Phrases (1983).

CHAPTER 1

Bernard Fosdyke knew just about enough German to order a drink and a meal, and anyhow the loudspeakers that were strung across the broad Berlin avenue facing the palace gave out only squeals and squawks interspersed with mumbles. The recipient of honour up on the balcony wore a morning coat that fitted badly at the back of the neck, with ill-set-in sleeves. He put Fosdyke in mind of a village carpenter in his Sunday best receiving the commendation of his lord and master for doing a particularly good job of fencing in the home paddock. The donor, on the other hand, in a grey uniform and a spiked helmet, delivered his mumbled peroration and handshake with the air of an old man whose mind and interests are elsewhere.

After the handshake of endorsement came the cheering and the slogan shouting, together with the forest of raised arm salutes. Fosdyke was fairly well hemmed in by the massed crowd. It had been raining since dawn, but the winter sun had broken through and folks were steaming inside their mackintoshes. Even out in the open air, the stench of body sweat was quote intolerable. Gently, by easy stages, and being particularly careful not to disturb anyone's raised hand or to give the appearance of a person who was bored with the proceedings, he managed to squirm his way to the edge of the crowd and make his way back towards his hotel, which was in a narrow street just off the Kurfürstendamm by the Kaiser Wilhelm Memorial Church.

He craved a cup of coffee, but all the cafés along the way —together with all shops, restaurants, tobacco kiosks and so forth—were closed by decree on the occasion of the induction of the new Chancellor, and furthermore, as Fosdyke's footsteps led him further away from the scene, he became aware that the streets had the appearance of a Sunday morning just after dawn, with not a soul in sight, not even a stray dog. All Berlin must be gathered in and around the palace; save for the halt, the lame and the blind—who, presumably, were listening to the proceedings huddled around the nearest available wireless set.

His passage echoing from the eyeless walls about him, Fosdyke presently came to the street where his hotel lay. He had barely turned the corner when he saw two big fellows in brown uniforms, jackboots, peaked caps, and the ubiquitous Nazi armbands. They gave him the immediate impression of being some kind of street patrol—which, indeed, was exactly what they were.

Well before Fosdyke reached them, they stopped, exchanged a few muttered words, nodded to each other, stood with their thumbs tucked into their belts, and awaited his approach, straddling the sidewalk—and blocking his passage.

'JUDE! HALT!'

The order came as he was half a dozen paces from them. The command was clear, the menace so tangible one could have cut it with a knife; and the repetition of the word *Jude*, as the speaker went into a harangue, was one of the few German words within the recipient's vocabulary.

'NA, WO GEHST DU HIN, JUDE?'

Now Fosdyke, whose maternal grandmother was Iberian-Irish, was what the British police dossiers of the time described as being 'of Jewish appearance', that is to say he possessed the dark-haired, blue-eyed ancestry of County Sligo, allied to the high-nosed, aristocratic profile of Aragón. And was frequently mistaken for one of the Chosen.

Not exactly a coward, but a man to whom violence, or the mere threat of violence, was a cause for alarm, Fosdyke perceived that he stood in error—from the viewpoint of the two storm-troopers—on two premises: one, that he was a

Jew and a German Jew at that; two, that he was committing
some sort of lèse-majesté by being out in the forsaken streets
when he should have been present at the ceremony, or—
more likely, this—hiding his alien face indoors.

He addressed himself to disabusing his challengers on
both counts.

'Look, I don't speak German, but I assure you I'm not
Jewish. And I've got a British passport here . . . ' He groped
for it.

The appeal did not have a pleasing effect; indeed, the
menace increased. The two storm-troopers unhooked their
thumbs from their belts and stepped towards him. Fosdyke
backed up against the wall.

'Er ist ein englischer Jude.'

'Englischer Scheissjude!'

Fosdyke raised his hands in a defensive gesture. 'Now,
look here, you chaps, I shall make very strong represen-
tations to my embassy about this, and you'll be in trouble
from your own authorities . . . '

He got no further. A knee in the groin and a punch in the
stomach doubled him up, choking. An elbow in the mouth,
and he felt one of his front teeth come loose. Next, he was
lying on the flagstones and they were kicking him with their
jackboots. He scarcely felt that, there being no room left in
his nervous system to record any more pain.

And then, through the mists of semi-consciousness, he saw
a bounding figure break into the scene. One of the brown-
shirted thugs was spun round by a massive hand. A flaxen-
haired head was brought forward to connect with a brutal
nose that had already been broken in some street fight or
other. The storm-trooper reeled back, collided with Fosdyke
while he was in the act of raising himself to his knees, and sent
the Englishman rocketing across the sidewalk and into the
gutter, where his hand came into connection with the barred
interstices of a drain cover. And stayed there.

The remainder of the scrimmage, which was between the

second storm-trooper (whose comrade had given up the struggle and lay whimpering face downwards in a puddle of nasal blood) and Fosdyke's strange rescuer (who, in addition to being blond, was also built on Viking lines) lasted no more than the time it took for Fosdyke to assess the tragedy of his own present condition. With fists, knees, feet, and another prod of his own blond, bullet head, the newcomer sent the Nazi thug sliding slowly backwards down the wall, to join his companion in adversity.

'Come on, feller,' said Fosdyke's rescuer, in the homely accents of the Bronx. 'Let's get the hell outa here and make some distance before these two fairies wake up and start hollering for Mama.'

'I—I can't move,' cried Fosdyke. 'I'm stuck here. You go—and thanks for what you did.'

'What do you mean, you can't move? Feller, if you stay here, it'll be a short sojourn in the local S.A. barracks for you, before they hand you over to the police on a charge of assault and battery—by which time, as regards physical shape, you'll be fit only for selling matches in the gutter, and I wouldn't give a nickel for your future means of procreation. And in parentheses I might add that the same would go for me also. 'So let's go—we both!'

'I've told you,' wailed Fosdyke. 'I'm stuck! My hand's stuck in the grating.'

'You are making mock of a simple young American, feller,' responded the big blond. 'But, on a point of information—show me.'

Fosdyke rolled aside, revealing his left hand, the four fingers of which were jammed into the grating as far as their second phalanges and in line with his signet ring.

'Now do you believe me?' he said.

The big American knelt, touched the hand, which was already swollen around the knuckles. He essayed a slight pull, which made Fosdyke scream out in agony, and one of the S.A. men stirred at the sound.

'I'd say that around—' the blond eyed Fosdyke over—
'around a hundred and ninety, two hundred pounds of good
bones, muscle and guts drove them fingers into that grating,
and it would take an equivalent weight, applied with a
similar force to the other end, to get 'em out. The means to
which we don't have here.'

'Then what am I going to *do*?' whispered Fosdyke, one
eye on the storm-troopers, who, it seemed to him, were on
the point of resuming interest in the world about them.

'Only one thing to do,' replied his companion. Whereupon, gingerly sticking the fingers of both his own hands
into the grating, he lifted the whole thing out by main force.
'You'll have to carry this goddamned hunk of old iron along
with you till we find a garage workshop or some such where
they can cut you out of it—or else a hospital where they
can extricate the fingers under general anaesthetic. And
neither of these two happy options is going to be available
to you in Germany. These two fairies saw us both quite
plainly. An hour from now, Berlin will be scoured for us.
The frontiers will be closed by midnight. And if they catch
us, the iron grating with *Berliner Stadtwerke* neatly inscribed
upon it in raised lettering, taken in conjunction with the
open drain, will clinch the matter as regards identity. They'll
lock us up and throw away the key. Let's go.'

'But—*where*?' demanded Fosdyke.

'Where's your hotel—where are you staying?'

Fosdyke told him.

The other peeled off his coat: a substantial tweed ulster.
'Wrap this kind of casually over your left forearm,' he said,
'so that it covers the hand and the grating both. The latter
you'll have to get used to carrying tucked under your arm.'

'It's heavy,' complained Fosdyke; he obeyed, notwithstanding.

'You'll get used to it,' said the other. 'Come on—my
automobile is just around the corner.'

Just around the corner was parked a massive Rolls-Royce

Silver Ghost coupé with the hood up. Fosdyke discerned that the rear seats were piled up with expensive-looking suitcases and cardboard crates.

'I'm checked out of the Bristol,' explained his rescuer, opening the front passenger door to enable him to get inside, iron grating and all. 'I'm heading west. Just happened to stop by to find someplace to buy a pack of cigarettes, when I heard you holler out.'

'For which I'm profoundly grateful,' responded Fosdyke. 'And I'm sorry you got involved.'

'We're *all* involved,' was the cryptic rejoinder. 'I more than you; but, brother, you and yours are gonna get deeply involved along with all the rest of us before you're much older.'

There being no ready-made response to such a declaration, Fosdyke let it pass. The Rolls had barely time to be shifted up and down its satin gearbox before they were gliding to a silent halt before the Englishman's hotel.

'I'll come up with you and help you pack,' said the American.

'Pack?' repeated Fosdyke, puzzled.

'You're coming alonger me, feller,' replied the other. 'Or you're a dead duck come breakfast time. Westwards we're driving, right through the night. To Paris, France, where a man can breathe the air of freedom—for the time being, anyhow.'

Fosdyke's room was one of the cheapest sort, looking out on to the kitchen yard area and all the garbage buckets. It did not even have the marginal benefit of a washbasin. The blond American helped him to pack his single cheap cardboard case. If he remarked the pile of battered notebooks, one shabby suit and a gallimaufry of mostly unwashed shirts and underwear that comprised his companion's slender belongings, he gave no sign. Fosdyke, incapacitated with only one hand, supervised the proceedings, while the

American shovelled the stuff into the suitcase, closed it, and, there being no lock, fastened a thick piece of string round it at the Englishman's direction.

'I don't even know your name,' said the latter. 'Mine's Fosdyke. Bernard Fosdyke.' He held out his right, free hand.

'And I'm Harold Hiram Levy,' responded the other. 'Glad to meet you, feller. Though it could have been in more auspicious circumstances. On the other hand, it's adversity that most always brings folks together. Take Christians being thrown to the lions in the Colosseum, or the event at the Little Big Horn on June 25, 1876, to name but two.'

'Levy?' repeated Fosdyke, puzzled, 'then you're a . . . a . . .'

'Sure, I'm a Yid,' replied the other cheerfully. 'And don't be taken in by the blue eyes and the riot of golden curls. We come in all shapes and sizes, colours and attitudes—just like everyone else.'

'They—the storm-troopers—mistook me for a Jew,' said Fosdyke.

'Nah!' responded Levy. 'You're a goddamned dago if I ever saw one. What? Italian?'

'English, actually—but part Spanish-Irish.'

'Any Yid would know you're not one of us,' said Levy. 'The give-away is the mouth, see?' He pointed to his own. 'When a Jew smiles, his lips turn up most excessively at the corners. This comes from smiling ingratiatingly when, for instance, some Cossack, having raped your daughter, is laying a knout across your back. It's a case of the law of natural selection. Darwin was right all the time. The Jews who didn't grin widely enough were eliminated. That left—us.'

He hefted the suitcase. 'Let's go, Bernard,' he said. 'We've got a long ways to drive before dawn.'

It was extraordinarily comfortable in the front passenger seat of the Rolls, and silent save for the ponderous ticking of the clock in the dashboard. Levy drove in the relaxed manner newly popularized by the motor-race aces: well back in his seat, arms extended and gripping the wheel loosely at ten to two. Along the arterial highways of North Germany, he seldom slowed below eighty miles an hour, and often touched a hundred—at which times Fosdyke cringed in his seat and his right foot strayed instinctively towards a phantom brake.

They did not speak. Presently, Fosdyke grew drowsy, waking from a semi-somnolent state when the Rolls slowed down to pass through a town; at which time, when the name sign of the place flashed past his window, he assembled a mental aide-memoire to fit it. Thus:

Brandenburg—Bach Concertos—easy.

Magdeburg—something about hemispheres—*hemispheres?* . . .

Halberstadt—name of a Boche aeroplane of the Great War?

Over the Harz mountains, so signposted—something about witches, surely . . .

A plaque announcing that they were about to cross the River Weser—Robert Browning and the Pied Piper.

He slept fitfully through Nordrhein-Westfalen, and did not see the fairyland of ice crystals touching every sprig of every branchlet of every tree in the wooded hills of winter, nor the sparkling, winding road that emptied itself forever before the fat tyres of the Rolls. He slept when they crossed the Rhine at Cologne, with the frowning spires of the great cathedral stark against the moon.

Levy woke him with a gentle nudge of the elbow.

'Feller, we're coming up to the frontier. Here's what we do. You sit with the coat over your lap and the hand and grating hidden. You give out the two passports to the officer—right? Keep a stiff upper lip, like you've got a bad smell under your nose. Look intransigently British. Do you get me?'

Fosdyke nodded. 'But what if they order us to get out of the car? What if—' the very concept made him shrink inside his skin— 'what if they strip and search us?'

'I haven't thought that right through yet,' replied his companion, 'but I'm working on it.'

Levy took a passport from the glove compartment, to which Fosdyke added his own. They made a couple of slow curves through woodland and small houses, all shuttered and sleeping. Then came a signpost: GRENZE—ZOLL. That —and a striped beam spanning the road beyond, and beckoning freedom.

An officer in a peaked cap approached. Behind him were two others in uniform; both had rifles slung over their shoulders. To Fosdyke's relief, their interrogator was smoothly pleasant. Considering his own circumstances— battered cardboard suitcase and reach-me-down suit—he was not to know that the newly post-Weimar Germany was ardently wooing well-heeled tourists, particularly rich foreigners in Rolls-Royces and the like. Particularly rich titled English tourists in Rolls-Royces.

A glance at their passports, and the functionary practically rolled over on his back and offered himself.

'Ach, so—Lord Aberathney, is it?'

Fosdyke opened his mouth to say something, or maybe emit a scream; it was his companion who answered, and in the loud and well-articulated accents of Eton and Oxbridge:

'Yes. I'm Aberathney. Any message for me from the British Consulate in Cologne?'

'I will go and see, my lord,' was the response.

'I should be most awfully obliged.'

The man went at a sharp trot towards a lighted hut nearby. The two armed guards remained. Fosdyke held himself tight. Presently the officer returned.

'No messages, my lord,' he reported.

'What a confounded nuisance,' replied Levy. 'This means I shall have to drive right through the demned night to reach Paris in time to catch the diplomatic bag to London. Ah well . . .'

The officer saluted and stood aside. 'Please proceed, my lord,' he said.

But Levy had not finished with his role. He leaned out of the driver's window and smiled foxily at the officer. Fosdyke's guts shrank within him.

'Officer, you haven't searched my baggage, nor that of my friend,' said Levy playfully. 'Which means you have missed the consignment of diamonds and art treasures that we are smuggling out of Germany.'

The other laughed nervously, uncertain of how to deal with this kind of English aristocrat, who, as he had gleaned from literature and Hollywood pictures, had as a class, by brutal inbreeding through near-incest, succumbed to an eccentricity that more nearly resembled insanity.

He waved them on. Saluted.

The barrier was raised by one of the armed guards. Another salute.

'We made it,' said Levy.

The way into France lay over a bridge across a stream, and another striped frontier post, which was opened in no great hurry by a functionary in a képi who had a cigarette dangling from his nether lip.

'You call yourself Lord Aberathney,' whispered Fosdyke in awe. 'But he's a big man in the . . .'

'It's useful, in my business,' replied Harold Hiram Levy, 'to take on a multitude of roles, a supply of assorted identities, with which to counter any specific problem that may arise. They're all in the glove compartment. Take your pick.'

There was a raft of passports inside the glove compartment: all British, all enjoining those inspecting, in the Name of His Britannic Majesty's Principal Secretary of State, et cetera, to allow the bearer to pass freely without let or hindrance, et cetera, et cetera . . .

Fosdyke riffled through them; read to himself the spurious declarations within, and wondered.

Professor Adrian Charles Fortescue–Browne. Occupation: Physicist.
Doctor Sir Hugh Mannering Clough. Occupation: Physician.
Mr Ernest Jago, MP. Occupation: Member of Parliament.
The Very Reverend Ignatius Manners, SJ. Occupation: Priest.
Mr Henry Higgins: Occupation: Retail fruiterer.

Fosdyke had no time to quiz his companion on the score of questions that teemed in his mind before the French frontier officer stuck his head through the window and, gusting the aromatic smoke of a Gauloise in their faces, demanded their passports. Fosdyke did not notice which his companion proffered by sleight of hand.

The Frenchman betrayed not the slightest interest in their documents: merely stamped them, using the back of his hand as a support, emitted another cloud of smoke and gestured them towards a kiosk marked: DOUANE.

The Customs officer, képi-ed and also smoking a Gauloise, eyed them both with a lacklustre, world-weary glance that he must have worked up from his impressions of the film actor Jean Gabin playing roles of a like nature.

'Avez-vous quelque chose à déclarer, messieurs?'

Relieved beyond belief, the nightmare of the S.A. barracks and all their multifarious accommodations dismissed from his mind, Fosdyke unwrapped his left hand and forearm and laid his burden on the table in front of the astonished functionary. It landed with a satisfyingly heavy clump.

'Only—*this*,' he declared.

Fosdyke slept upon their departure. When he awoke, the signposts were promising *Paris—40 km*, and progressively better.

It was still dark, but promised a lively dawn, and frosty.

He shivered inside his crumpled tweeds. Some day, he thought, there must be a fortune for the chap who invents some sort of interior heating for motor-cars.

The unlovely landscape of Northern France, its architectural heritage not greatly improved by the dogged, dreadful war that had raged over it only fifteen years previously, came to light in the sullen, fitful dawn.

Presently, Fosdyke said: 'You puzzled me back there, Levy. I mean, what do you really *do* for a living that calls for the—surely awfully risky—business of posing as half a dozen or so—well—awfully disparate sorts of chap? I merely ask. It isn't any part of my business. Only—I have this special bond with you.

'After all, you saved a very big part of my life. And my freedom. And very much else, perhaps. So I feel that the bond you have established makes me free to plead your confidence. Do I have it right?'

'Sure,' responded the other cheerfully. 'It's no secret. I'm in the art-dealing business. My interest in Berlin lay in a particular picture in the National Gallery, that, following upon the elevation of the house-painter Hitler to the Chancellorship of one of Europe's primary sources of culture, has already been deemed to be unsuitable for display to decent, family-loving Aryans, and has consequently been relegated to the cellars on account of it depicts a Jewish rabbi—though painted by the immortal hand of Rembrandt. I have—had—a certain interest in acquiring the painting.'

'Oh yes?' said Fosdyke, puzzled.

'I applied to the director of the gallery to be permitted to view the work in question, be it in the cellars or wherever. He took a look at the name I was using—Henry Higgins—and excused himself to make a phone call. I so far abrogated my habitual civility as to put my ear to the door to listen in on his end of the call. He was talking to someone at Nazi party headquarters about me. Which is why I checked out of the Bristol in a hurry—and why we're here . . . How's your hand?'

'Hurts.'

'We'll stop off and get you out of that Berlin rat trap just as soon as daylight breaks, Bernard. Now, tell me—what do you do for a living, and how come you were in Berlin? You surely weren't there on account of Hitler's induction as Reich Chancellor.'

'Oh no,' said Fosdyke. 'I'm a writer—a novelist. I went to Berlin because, as I understood, it's the place where the artistic activity is so lively. I went—as it were—looking for colour.'

'Colour?' Levy laughed shortly. 'Feller, I bet you found plenty of colour in the bars off the Kurfürstendamm.'

Bernard Fosdyke met his reflection in the vanity mirror above his head, and discovered that he was blushing with embarrassment.

'Well, as a matter of fact—yes,' he admitted. 'To be honest with you—um—Harold, I've never seen anything like it—or even dreamed of anything like it—in all my life. You see, I didn't have the advantage of boarding at an English boys' public school.'

Bernard Fosdyke had been born in 1901 in a slate-grey Midlands city which was already far into industrial decline; though no one guessed, then, how far the decline would go. We still had the Empire upon which the sun never set, didn't we? Every Empire Day, the kids waved Union Jacks and sang: 'Wider still, and wider, shall thy bounds be set/ God, who made thee mighty/ Make thee mightier yet!' Not a dry eye in the place.

A highly-strung, nervous child and inclined to be 'chesty', Bernard was spared the horrors of boarding at the expensive so-called 'public school' where his father had spent four immeasurably miserable years—and these same short-comings would also have kept him from the holocaust of the Great War, even if he had not still been a year below military age at the Armistice.

The Fosdykes were of the prosperous middle class.

Fosdyke père, an inventor and entrepreneur of some small genius, had made a considerable fortune by devising a new means of weaving elastic thread into lace to support ladies' knickers, in the course of which enterprise he did a tremendous amount of practical field work in the cocktail bars and nightclubs of London's West End. The firm to whom he sold the patent offered Fosdyke senior the option of a lump sum or half the amount and a small piece of the action. Never prudent, Fosdyke elected for the bird in the hand. Two years later (and Bernard was sixteen at the time), slow horses, fast women and whisky saw him off.

In the days of their relative prosperity, the family had lived in a rather splendid Edwardian mansion in an exclusive district of the city, with a formal garden, a fernery, a three-car garage, four living-in servants and two dailies. Bernard, reduced by his poor health to minimal education (he had to take a nap every afternoon) was hand-walked daily by his nanny to a neighbourhood private school which was co-educational. This last factor—being brought into close contact at an impressionable age with members of the opposite sex—possibly had a profound effect upon Bernard's subsequent emotional development, giving him the deeply ingrained suspicion of, and a profound fear of, womankind in general.

Following upon the untimely death of his profligate father, the collapse of the family fortunes and the subsequent demise of his mother, Bernard was left with the legacy of the Edwardian mansion, which nobody wanted to buy in the time of the worldwide depression, and which was mortgaged to the hilt anyhow. He eased his way out of this particular difficulty by renting the place to an order of Anglican teaching nuns who set up a kindergarten school there. From this slender rent, which serviced the mortgage repayments, he also gleaned the sum of fifteen pounds a month to live on. The employment market had no place for the likes of him in the cut-throat post-war period.

It was then, when it seemed that his chances were at an

all-time low, that he saw—*the advertisement* . . .

WHAT HAVE ALL THESE IN COMMON ? ? ?

KIPLING
MARK TWAIN
HALL CAINE
COLETTE
E. RICE-BURROUGHS
ELINOR GLYN
OUIDA
EDGAR WALLACE
and
YOU

The answer to this very simple question is that all
these *famous, rich and successful* authors have done no
more than REALIZE THEIR POTENTIAL ACHIEVEMENT.
We are all WRITERS! Last week, you wrote a
letter to a friend or relation. That is the present
height of your achievement. Why not build upon
your potential and master the FEW AND SIMPLE
RULES of the writers' craft?
Fill in the form below. NO OBLIGATION.

The Authors' College
15a Green Street
Birmingham.
Please send me a copy of your brochure: *Be a
Successful Author in 12 Months*. FREE!
Name . . . .
Address . . . .
. . . .
. . . .

The notorious advertising standards of the times being

what they were, Bernard Fosdyke was well aware of the catchpenny nature of the insert. However, he had a leaning towards the literary life and had written several short stories and essays in a twopenny notebook, which he had never shown to anyone—dully conscious as he was of his lack of formal instruction in the English language.

Not, then, falling completely 'hook, line and sinker', as the saying is, he filled in the form and sent it off in the hope that The Authors' College might provide him with the essential ingredients for composing English prose that had been denied him in more rigorous, formal education.

By return of post, back came a most encouraging document, setting out a regimen of home-learning by mail. And all at a cost of only five guineas. This seemed to Fosdyke to be a modest and reasonable outlay, and he sent off his cheque.

Again by return there came a slim, papercovered volume setting out in very simple terms the rules of English composition. The instructions ended with a short examination which included an essay on a set subject. It was the latter which won for him a most glowing appreciation from the college principal—one Ambrose S. Featherstonehaugh—in a letter with a closing paragraph that had Fosdyke doing entrechats up and down his narrow kitchen in darkest Pimlico:

> . . . in short, I offer you a partnership in my enterprise, where, for the small consideration of an investment in the College, you will be an equal with myself, and be provided with a sheet anchor of a steady and lucrative income while still pursuing a literary career that cannot fail to bring you both fame and fortune. Remember, do, that Mr T. S. Eliot, perhaps our most distinguished poet, still combines the role of editor with that of revitalizing English verse in all regards . . .

It was the nod in the direction of T. S. Eliot that did it.

Fosdyke, inspired by the vision of a brilliant future that included fame, fortune and the love of complaisant women, went to see Mr Featherstonehaugh at the College—first arranging matters with his bank manager so that he was granted the facility of a loan of £1500, repayable in monthly instalments of £15 over eight years and a bit—the residual of the rental from his family house, and his sole source of income.

The Principal of the Authors' College was an individual whose manner and bearing, indeed his whole demeanour, dress, manicurage, the very scent of his personal cologne (brave but not demanding), were of the sort to inspire immediate trust and respect. Someone more worldly than Bernard Fosdyke might have cavilled that the red silk handkerchief which overspilled the breast pocket of the suavely-waisted and undoubtedly Savile-Row-tailored pin-striped suit did so somewhat over-exuberantly; that the red carnation which adorned the buttonhole was a trifle too pink in the shade; and an even severer critic could have made out a good case against the tie which was sprinkled with the escutcheon of Cambridge University ('Why, my dear Watson, does he not commit himself by wearing the tie of his particular college? Why the sweeping generality?')

The unworldly Fosdyke (who frankly admitted to being a 'bird in the wilderness' in business matters—a view shared by his bank manager), was so impressed that he there and then wrote a cheque for fifteen hundred pounds (the least that Featherstonehaugh would accept—having gleaned that it was all Fosdyke had), making it out to cash and uncrossed, and departed rejoicing—with a pile of college students' exam papers to correct: a proud chore, proudly borne.

He never saw or heard of Ambrose S. Featherstonehaugh again. It later transpired that 15a Green Street was an accommodation address, rented by the day or week. After mulcting half a dozen other such would-be littérateurs as

Fosdyke, the Principal of the Authors' College departed to Monte Carlo for the summer season, to play The Millionaire South American Widower trick and The Blinded Air Ace in Need of an Operation trick.

It was Fosdyke's first brush with the world of confidence trickery—but, as will be seen, by no means his last.

CHAPTER 2

The grating was removed from Bernard Fosdyke's hand by a sullen garage owner in a village just east of Compiègne, who cut through the bars with a hacksaw; expressing not the slightest curiosity or interest as to how the thing came to be there; taking a five-franc piece in payment and biting upon it in the manner of peasantry the world over who suppose that smart-alecks from the big city are all crooks.

Levy claimed the grating and laid it in the back of the Rolls.

'You might care to hang on to that,' he said. 'Frame it and put it up over the fireplace. Almost a momento mori, you might say.'

Fosdyke shuddered.

They breakfasted in a café in Compiène: excellent coffee in deep bowls, freshly-baked croissants, farm butter, over-sweetened apricot jam. Levy ordered a large Scotch whisky. He then carefully tutored the proprietor in the art of pouring it into a tall tumbler filled with ice. This he drank in three long draughts immediately he had finished his coffee and croissants.

'I think I could fancy one of those,' said Fosdyke. 'It's been quite a night.'

In fact, they had two each.

'What are you going to do from here in, Bernie?' asked Levy. 'I take it that I may so address you?'

'No one else has done so in that particular contraction,' responded Fosdyke, 'but a man who has arguably saved the larger part of my life expectation has a certain lien on my good will. Might I in turn call you Harry?'

'Hal I much prefer,' responded the other.

'Hal it is,' said Fosdyke. 'As to my immediate future, that's uncertain. As I told you, I went to Berlin to collect background for the definitive novel of the nineteen-thirties, since it is there that the new English writers are gathering this year to soak up the tremendous atmosphere of culture; for Germany is leading, so they say, in the theatre, in film-making, the modern novel, all aspects of the arts. It's to be hoped that the Nazis don't spoil everything. 'I regret to say, however, that apart from a rather unpleasant episode in a bar off the Kurfürstendamm, I added nothing to my experience. This was possibly because I speak no German.'

'French—you speak pretty good French. I heard you snorting away at the garage guy when he got a mite rough with his hacksaw.'

'Yes, I had a French nanny when I was a child. She was strongly Anglophobe, so I got the hang of French pretty early on. Unfortunately, my mother caught Hortense and Father engaged in some sort of entente cordiale. I was only seven at the time, so my French has never really progressed beyond nursery chit-chat. What I mean is, I can't cuss and swear in the vernacular, though I can outsmart most seven-year-old Frogs.

Levy laughed. 'Bernie, I think you're kidding me a little.'

Fosdyke smilingly conceded this gentle imputation, and privately attributed his flippancy to the excessive Scotch. 'I think I'd rather like another of those,' he added. 'As I was replying in answer to your question, the—um—Berlin project having been a failure, I was contemplating my departure from there when our present little trouble blew up. There were, however, slight snags in the way . . .'

'What snags were these, Bernie?'

'Well, one snag, really,' replied Fosdyke. 'I calculated that, when I had paid my hotel bill at the end of this current week, I shouldn't have enough money to buy my ticket home to England.'

'I see,' said Levy. 'In other words, you're broke.'

'Stony broke,' confirmed the other, and sighed into the dregs of his Scotch, which he then immediately swallowed down. 'In fact, discounting my share of this excellent liquid breakfast, I reckon that I have about two pounds, fifteen shillings and sixpence sterling to my name.'

'It's not a lot,' said Levy. 'But it will see you through a couple of days in Paris. That is, if you don't eat. Drink a little—but don't eat. And after that?'

'Well, I have the manuscript of an eighty-thousand-word novel with a London publisher,' said Fosdyke. 'Of which I have great hopes.'

'Really? What is the plot of this novel?' asked the other. 'If I may so far presume to intrude upon the interior mystery of a work of art that is certain to have the English-speaking world rioting in the bookshops and lending libraries.'

If there was irony intended in the question, Fosdyke did not appear to notice it. 'Well—er—Hal,' he said, 'it's about this chap who ostensibly discovers a way to turn water into petrol—that's to say, gasoline—by the simple means of adding a solution of his own devising. Just a few drops to every pint. He's an organic chemist, you see. Quite high up in the profession. A Cambridge don.'

'I like it,' said Levy. 'If I may anticipate the next move in the plot, I would say that the oil companies of the Western world, the real fat cats, bid for this invention, and for one reason—to bury it a hundred feet underground, wrapped around in concrete. Right?'

'That's right,' replied Fosdyke. 'Only, our friend Murdoch—that's the hero's name—won't part with the invention. Instead, he leads them on. Gives demonstrations of the principle to the Royal Society, the Imperial College of Science, seminars at both Oxford and Cambridge, the Sorbonne, Harvard and Yale—at the end of which demonstrations, the gleeful chairmen presiding ride home in their Rollses, their Cadillacs, their Bugattis—on a gallon beaker of Murdoch's jazzed-up water that had been prepared before their very eyes.'

'Don't tell me what happens next,' interposed Levy, by this time clearly enthused. 'Let me guess. The big oil cartels, fearful of seeing their massive empires almost literally going up in a puff of Murdoch's exhaust smoke, decide to gang together, bring in some hit men to rub out Murdoch and destroy his formula. Right?'

Fosdyke nodded. 'Basically, that part—the action and suspense—forms the greater part of the book,' he said. 'But Murdoch, anticipating this, defeats all their stratagems. He sells out to the United States Government and disappears from sight—in fact, to a paradise isle in the South Seas.'

'But the formula, I take it—that was a fake?'

Of course,' said Fosdyke. 'The whole thing was a confidence trick.'

'But—how?' demanded Levy. 'Okay, he scared all hell out of the oil cartels—these are mostly headed by guys whose thoughts seldom progress higher than their next yacht and the acquisition of a new showgirl or two. But how does Murdoch fool the Royal Society and all points west? Explain me that.'

'I do it in a short coda at the end of the book,' replied Fosdyke. 'When he was a very little boy, his favourite aunt gave Murdoch an Every Boy's Own Illusionist Set, in which was revealed the means to turn red-tinted water into blue and vice versa, how to produce handkerchiefs out of people's ears—things of that ilk. Murdoch simply built on the enthusiasm that his aunt's present had kindled. He became possibly one of the finest illusionists of his generation. But all the time he kept this a secret. His whole life—the hours interminable that he spent practising in front of the mirror in his locked bedroom, the hard slogging he put into becoming a top organic chemist—was all directed to one end: to win for himself a paradise island in the South Seas, and all that went with it.'

Levy was silent for quite a long while, but all the time regarding his companion. He drained his glass, signalled to the patron for a refill for them both.

Presently he said: 'You know what, Bernie? What you have told me—the plot of this novel that you have succinctly revealed to me—indicates one thing about your character that you have maybe not even registered in your own mind.'

'And what's that?' asked Fosdyke, amused.

'You have a fundamentally criminal personality,' rejoined Levy. 'That's to say, you have a basic amorality, a subtle and a guileful imagination. Do I offend you?'

'By no means, my dear chap,' responded Fosdyke, laughing. 'It's just the thought that, with all my subtlety and guile, I should by now have made a better thing of my life. And certainly not have let myself be so brazenly cheated as I have been on one occasion.' He was thinking of Mr Featherstonehaugh and The Authors' College—and his laughter faded as he gazed down into the icy depths of his drink.

They were silent for a while, and then Levy said: 'Bernie, I believe that you are the guy whom I've been looking for. Do you know Paris?'

'Scarcely,' replied Fosdyke. 'I was taken there when young, but Paris as the City of Light, the Sin Capital of Europe and all that—it quite passed me by as a boy of nine. Why do you ask, Hal—and why am I the guy you've been looking for, and for what, pray?'

For answer, Levy took out a pocket book, in which he scribbled a few lines, talking as he went. 'I'll drop you outside a clean, cheap hotel right off the Boulevard St-Michel,' he said, 'that won't strain the resources of your two pounds fifteen shillings and sixpence overmuch. Get yourself a good night's sleep, and meet me tomorrow noon at the Café des Deux Magots, a haunt much favoured by artists, writers, intellectuals and similar phonies, which stands on a corner of the Boulevard St-Germain right opposite the church of St-Germain-des-Prés. You can't miss it.' He tore out the page that gave Fosdyke the names and directions.

Now, Bernard Fosdyke had in the intervening years established in his mind a premise—entirely erroneous—that The Authors' College disaster had been a lesson well learned, and that he would never again be taken in by a smooth line of patter and the siren call of profit. He was ruminating on this when his companion, having called for the score, paid for it from a thick roll of notes of many denominations and currencies, topping it off with a handsome tip that even brought a smile of avarice if not of gratitude to the lugubrious face of the patron.

Taken all in all—the Rolls-Royce Silver Ghost, the impeccable matched crocodile-skin baggage, the bankroll so lightly borne—his companion suggested an affluence that surely could have no designs upon his, Fosdyke's, pathetic widow's mite: the two pounds, fifteen shillings and sixpence that stood between him and the workhouse. On the other hand, the deck of fake passports, the unseemly haste in which, even before the encounter with the S.A. bully-boys, Levy had been planning to leave Germany, gave some cause for doubt.

He decided to express that doubt. Three if not four Scotches on the rocks dictated the slightly forceful manner of address:

'What exactly are we going to discuss at our meeting tomorrow, my dear Hal?' he demanded.

'Making a fortune,' replied the other. And would not be drawn further.

The unseasonably bright sun and relative warmth of the following midday had inspired some of the cafés along the boulevards to strip down their glass partitions as if for summer; some of their clientèle, indeed, had advantaged themselves of this delicate suggestion of warmer days ahead; at the Café des Deux Magots, the establishment's sidewalk area was firmly enclosed in shuttered glass that, from the outside, betrayed nothing of its interior save a thick coating of vapourized breath, behind which vague forms wavered to and fro like goldfish in a murky tank.

When Fosdyke arrived at the café (five minutes before noon, after a good night's sleep, a late lie-in and an extremely hot but agonizingly confined bath), he was met by a gusting of tobacco smoke, shrill cries of waiters, loud chit-chat from the clientèle, and the leitmotif of garlic. He took his place at an empty table for two, after checking around that Levy had not yet arrived. There were two personages at the next table. One of them—sixtyish, grey hair cut en brosse, rasping deep voice of Transatlantic timbre—put him in mind of a meat porter, or maybe a dock worker. The other, whose back was turned to him, wore thick tweeds and said nothing in reply to the other's peroration.

'Alice, I'm worried about Pablo. Maybe he went straight to the apartment. Give it a quarter-hour and then I think you take a cab back to the Rue de Fleurus and check that the poor darling isn't waiting outside there in the cold. Come to think of it, save the cab fare and take a walk there. The exercise will do you good.'

It was then, with a slight frisson, that Fosdyke discerned the meat porter cum dock worker to be a woman.

To Fosdyke's left, sitting alone, a man in his early forties was hunched over a notebook, in which, between frequent delves into a cognac glass, he addressed himself to a feverish scribbling. The manner of his doing so—the occasional darting glances about him, his habit of covertly closing the notebook whenever folks passed close to him, or the waiter came to replenish his glass—gave Fosdyke the impression that he must be some sort of spy, or perhaps a divorce detective writing up his nocturnal report of watching lights go out in bedroom windows. The Englishman was speculating upon this when a gust of chilly wind heralded the entrance of his new friend Harold Hiram Levy. He wore a dark red carnation buttonhole.

'How's it with you, Bernie?' asked the latter, sitting himself down. 'How's the hotel?'

'It's quite clean and comfortable after its fashion, Hal,' responded the other. 'I was a bit puzzled by the rather colourful ladies who were lolling in the doorway when I came back from getting myself a modest supper at the brasserie down the street, but the to-ing and fro-ing up and down the stairs all through the night, not to mention the sounds through the paper-thin walls on both sides of my room, explained all that. What are you going to have to drink?'

They both had Scotch on the rocks.

'Bottoms up—first today,' said Levy.

'Your very good health,' responded Fosdyke. 'And now—do we talk about this intriguing suggestion of yours about making a fortune? I should tell you, my dear fellow, that, in the dark hours of the night—kept awake as I was by the romantic transactions next door on both sides—I decided that the only solution to my immediate financial problem is to commit some minor crime in France and have myself sentenced to enforced board and lodgings by the Third Republic.'

The big blond American grinned. 'That isn't going to be necessary, Bernie,' he said. 'Look around you as we sit here. This joint is patronized by the avant-garde art and literary establishment of the decade, whose only contribution to art and literature—in my humble opinion—is to perpetuate a myth which they themselves have propagated. Call me Philistine if you will—I see the name framing on your lips . . .'

'By no means, my dear Hal,' Fosdyke reassured him. 'I

have had some small contact with similar coteries in London. Bloomsbury is a seething mass of artistic pretension, so are the outer purlieus of Harrogate and Bradford, while Chelsea—surprisingly, considering its reputation during the period of Wilde, Whistler and the rest—is now the most favoured residential area of young gentlemen who do something in the City connected with the Stock Exchange, Lloyd's, merchant banking, the Baltic Exchange, et cetera; who depart in top hats every morning at nine, kissing their little wives goodbye, and return at five-thirty to put on their slippers and listen to the wireless set. But to return to artistic pretension: I have seen a lot of it and am entirely in sympathy with your views.' He looked about him. 'Assuming that your denunciation of the art and literary establishment here present is somehow connected with your plan to make a fortune for us both—' he looked anxiously at his companion—'I *assume* that you mean us both? . . .'

'Us both,' responded Levy.

'Then, please, give me a verbal conducted tour of these personages,' said Fosdyke, taking another deep quaff of his iced Scotch. Really, the prospect of becoming an enforced guest of the French Republic and being deprived of booze was almost too awful to contemplate.

'Immediately in front of us, at the next table,' said Levy, sotto voce, 'is the dame with the cropped grey hair. Now she is a person of my own ethnic and religious persuasion. An American citizen, moreover, but ruggedly expatriate. Posing as a littérateur—call it littérateuse at a stretch— dear Gertrude, who has an insatiable appetite for people of the artistic bent, plus an independent income, has espoused the careers of artists and writers interminable, myself included—for a time.' So saying, he met the eyes of the woman in question; was greeted with a puzzled glance, a moment of unenthusiastic recognition, a curt nod, and a look away.

'I think I should go find Pablo,' said her companion in a whiny voice. 'But I'd like another drink first. Something different. What do you suggest, Gertrude?'

'Drink is a drink is a drink,' was the enigmatic response.

'Coming in now,' said Levy, as the briefly opened door brought a fresh infusion of icy air, 'is another fellow American who last year published a book about the Spanish bullfight. He's also one of Gertrude's protégés and I guess he will now go over to join her and Alice. No—he's pausing to have a mocking word with Henry, who's something of a joke around the expatriate American intellectuals in Paris, since he's engaged in writing a filthy book that's not going to get published this side of Doomsday. Just listen to the chit-chat . . .'

The newcomer, a burly man in a broad-brimmed fedora and carrying a pile of books tied up with string, paused by the table of the man whom Fosdyke had noted earlier; who looked up with some irritation from his notebook as he was addressed with a somewhat mocking tone by the new arrival: 'Well, hello, Brother Miller. And how's it going? Got yourself a publisher?'

'Yes, I think so, Ernest.'

'Got a title yet?'

'Yes.'

'What?'

'Goddamnit, wait and see!'

'That's a great title, Henry.' Amused, the burly man went on to the table where the grey-haired woman, rising, kissed him on both cheeks and dragged him down to sit beside her.

'Stick around a little longer and you'll see more of them,' said Levy. 'That table over there—the one with the reservation tag on it—that's where Jean Cocteau holds court most lunch-times. He's just finished making an avant-garde motion picture right now. The point I am trying to make, Bernie . . .'

'The point you are trying to make, Hal,' prompted Fosdyke, 'is that these people—the artists, writers, intellectuals and (as you rate them) phonies—comprise the concerted hegemony in defiance of whom, and by some means, you plan to make fortunes for us both. Do I have it right?'

The big American leaned back in his seat and eyed his companion with the air of a man who has suddenly found himself in charge of a chimpanzee who has not only played the theme of the final movement of Beethoven's Ninth Symphony right through, but has scored it for full orchestra and voices. With riffs.

'You are remarkably prescient, Bernie,' he observed. 'You have it substantially right. Your no doubt élite and expensive education sits well upon you.'

'Education had I little,' responded the other, 'but I am of the persuasion that will happily peruse the small print on lavatory paper when nothing else offers itself. I am extremely well-read.'

'Well, then,' said Levy. 'We will make a million, and it would be a pleasant irony to do so with the help of these here assembled, their confrères and consœurs in—as you inform me—Bloomsbury, Harrogate and Bradford; taking in, from my own observations, a large part of Greenwich Village, certain purlieus of Charleston, South Carolina, and that part of Hollywood which apes the cinéastic pretensions of Berlin.'

A sour-faced Ganymede having been summoned and their cups refilled, Fosdyke asked: 'What is this plan, Hal—and where and how do we begin?'

'To begin,' said his companion, 'we must first make a judicious survey of certain opinions among those whom pundits have begun to describe as "The Man in the Street". This you will carry out, Bernie, commencing this afternoon. The matter is very simple: standing on street corners at selective places in Paris that I have marked in this excellent street guide, you will pose two simple questions to all comers, quite unselectively, be they man, woman, black, white, French, Eskimo, or whatever. What I need, my dear Bernie, is to test out a theory which I have. That being done, we can proceed with the next part of the plan—which, all being well, I shall reveal to you this evening. Here. Eight o'clock.'

'Can you tell me no more?' asked Fosdyke. 'Hal, I must confess to you that I am greatly embarrassed financially. But this you must know because I have made no secret of it . . . and the patron of the hotel has already intimated that my slender luggage is no security beyond an overnight stay.'

'Say no more, my dear feller,' responded the other, and took from his hip pocket the stout roll of banknotes, from which he stripped three hundred francs in fifties. 'This will keep you in some style till we have devised a permanent arrangement.'

'Well, thanks, but . . .' began Fosdyke.

'I have to go now,' said Levy, rising. 'Stick around here. Listen to the phoney chit-chat, and maybe have a bite to eat. After that, get out there into the streets and begin your survey.'

'But—this survey,' said Fosdyke, panicking slightly. 'What do I *ask* this conglomerate Man in the Street?'

'It's in this envelope,' said the other, dropping an envelope on the table top by Fosdyke's elbow. 'See you this evening at eight.'

A wave—and he was gone in another cold draught.

After committing some of his new-found affluence to another Scotch, and with the parakeet chatter resounding all about him, Fosdyke gingerly addressed himself to the contents of the envelope, and found inside a sheet of lined notepaper bearing on one side only a message in terse typescript. As follows:

THE SELECTED PLACES on the street map where you carry out your survey are all situated in tourist Paris and solid bourgeois Paris—not in the bohemian area of the Left Bank where you are now sitting, Bernie.

LOCATIONS. Commencing at the corner with the Place de la Concorde, patrol the left-hand side of the Rue Royale as far as the Madeleine and back. Pick twenty subjects at random. Then move on.

NEXT. The whole length of the Champs Elysées on the right-hand side up to the Place de L'Etoile. From there, take the Avenue de Friedland and the Boulevard Haussmann . . . (*There followed an itinerary that would bring Fosdyke on a zigzag course along the grands boulevards through the 9th and 10th arrondissements, taking in the areas of the tourists, boulevardiers, flâneurs, and more solid citizenry.*)

THE QUESTIONS YOU WILL ASK:

(1) What is the most famous painting in the Paris Louvre museum?

(2) What is the *next* most famous painting in the said museum?

That was all that Levy provided; no explanations, no asides, no comments; just the bald instructions. It seemed to Fosdyke, on the face of it, to be a not too arduous task, though perhaps promising to be a bit hard on the feet.

Sipping his drink, he supposed that Levy knew what he was up to, and would be more confiding in the particulars of his intentions when their relationship—partnership?—was more clearly defined. Meanwhile, the other having not only saved him from an extremely nasty situation in Berlin, but having also staked him to three hundred francs without question, must certainly have his trust in Bernard Fosdyke fulfilled.

Fosdyke paid his bill, just as the fussy lady named Alice departed from her friends to seek out the missing Pablo whoever. The Englishman folded up his instructions and put them in his side pocket along with the street guide. A taxi, he decided, would most conveniently take him to the Place de la Concorde and the beginning of his Paris Odyssey. After that it would be Shanks's Pony.

CHAPTER 3

The Place de la Concorde, when Fosdyke paid off his cab, was under a flurry of fine snow. A party of schoolgirls, with a nun in the van and another in the rear, were crossing over to the central island, cloaks flowing like bats' wings under the protecting arm of a grinning agent de police. It was not, thought Fosdyke, the sort of day for buttonholing perfect strangers in the streets and quizzing them about their aesthetic inclinations.

To work, however, to work!

Twenty yards up the Rue Royale there emerged from the doors of the famed Maxim's restaurant a lady and gentleman whose manner, bearing and attire declared them to be English—or, possibly, Scottish—of the very highest social sort. He was in expensive but well-worn tweeds and a deerstalker hat, as befitted the weather. She was in furs, and a cloche hat of veteran provenance. Both had the high colour, the pominent facial bone structures, the spare and elongated physiques that told of centuries of interbreeding, interminable hours spent in the saddle, on grouse moors in frost, or wading thigh-deep in torrential salmon rivers in streaming rain; and wearing expressions that betokened belief in Empire and the White Man's Burden.

'Excuse me, sir,' began Fosdyke. 'May I ask you a couple of questions, please?'

'A couple of *questions*?' The mild inquiry brought a flash of something like affront to the pale blue eyes, whose vision was immediately augmented by the addition of a gold-rimmed monocle attached to black ribbon, through which added vantage the wearer regarded his addressor from head to foot and back again. 'A couple of questions? What questions are *these*? Questions relating to *what*, pray?'

'The man must have quite lawst his wits,' declared the lady. 'What bloody presumption.'

'I—um—it's about your taste in Art,' said Fosdyke. 'I'm —er—doing a survey, you see.'

'In—*Art?*' The couple stared at each other, and the man allowed his monocle to fall, more or less of its own accord, to the full extent of its ribbon, where it swung, pendulum-wise, till the law of Newton and Gravity took over.

'Art,' repeated Fosdyke.

'And what have *we* to do with—Art?' demanded the man. 'For that matter, what are you doing in these foreign parts —since one presumes from your accent that you are an Englishman—accosting persons with whom you have not the slightest acquaintance in the public street? Are you a Bolshevik revolutionary? There is no other explanation for your appalling incivility.'

'No, I'm not, sir,' responded Fosdyke, backing away. 'And I'm terribly sorry to have troubled you in this manner. Good day to you.'

He fled.

Clear upon the freezing air, their comments followed him as he went on up the Rue Royale:

'Bloody Bolsheviks—they're everywhere. Be voted into the Carlton Club next, I shouldn't wonder.'

'They should be taken out,' declared the woman dis-passionately, but in a voice that would have carried like a bell across a fifty-acre stretch of grouse moor, 'and shot in batches of six or a dozen.'

That's a fine start, thought Fosdyke. Why did I have to come across a pair of upper-class English loonies first off?

He slowed his pace as he came abreast of the next culinary establishment along the street: a café of reasonably fine pretensions. He craved for a scalding hot cup of coffee laced with Scotch. But duty called. Coming towards him was a young woman dressed in a woolly coat with a woolly hat pulled down over her brow and ears and almost entirely hiding her dark hair, which showed only in curling flicks at cheeks and turned up about her neck. Her face was healthily pink, lips generously full and lightly rouged. And she walked with a purposeful swing.

'Excusez-moi, mam'selle. Je vous en prie . . .'

'English?' she demanded, raising an eyebrow but looking not in any way offended at being accosted.

'Yes,' said Fosdyke. 'I'm doing a survey—about artistic tastes. I'm—um—doing it for the Louvre museum.' (As well concoct some sort of sales patter, if that was the expression, to spare one from the sort of indignity he had just suffered.)

'But how terribly interesting,' she replied. 'Look—it's much too cold to stand out here. I'm going in for a hot drink. Why don't you come in out of the wind and snow and put your questions to me in comfort?'

Why not, indeed? And why, when she had taken her place at a table for two, should he not take the other seat; and why, having done so, should he not adopt the role of host and boldly ask her what she would like to drink, and he was having a coffee with a Scotch—nothing like that to keep out the frost. They both laughed, and she said she'd have the same.

'My name's Fosdyke,' he said. 'Bernard Fosdyke.'

'I'm Dorothy Batthyány.'

'You'll have to say that again,' he said.

She said it again. 'It's Hungarian,' she added.

'Then you're Hungarian?' She had the most beautiful eyes, he thought. A fugitive blue that faded into deep violet as she turned her head away from the light.

'More than that, I'm American-Irish-Hungarian,' she said. 'And what do you do when you're not picking up girls in the Rue Royale with a dubious story about doing surveys on people's artistic tastes for the Louvre?'

'It's quite true,' he said. 'I am doing a survey. In fact, I started only today. You're my second customer. How about that?'

'Marvellous! How did you cope with your first customer?'

He told her about the English couple, and that kept them laughing till the coffee and Scotch were brought. He showed her how to decant the jigger of spirit into the coffee cup after giving the latter a firm stir.

'You're good at that,' she said. 'Do you put in a lot of practice?'

'I certainly imbibe occasionally,' admitted Fosdyke. 'There are some who'd call me a boozer.'

'You can't be that,' she said, 'or you wouldn't own up to it. You're what my Irish grandfather on my mother's side would have called "a feller who likes a drop". That's all.'

'You're kinder than you know,' he said.

Their eyes met, and he was the first to look away.

'Tell me about this survey,' she said.

'Well, I have to ask you two questions,' said Fosdyke, taking out the cheap notebook that he had bought in the Boulevard St Germain.

'Fire away.'

'Um—what is the most famous painting in the Paris Louvre museum? That's the first question.'

She frowned. Her hands—most remarkably small and well-shaped hands, thought Fosdyke, who had never considered himself an authority on female hands—reached up and touched her chin, her rounded cheeks.

'I don't think I can answer that,' she replied. 'You see— I'm not very familiar with the Louvre, which seems to me to be a rather dead place, like a marble vault where folks go to regard the splendid monuments to their ancestors. And Art isn't a bit like that—though, don't mistake me, I'm no artist, I'm a student of human nature, and that's all. No pretensions. But . . .'

'But?' he asked. She really was a most divinely lovely creature.

'Do you know the Rodin museum, Mr Fosdyke?'

'No, I'm afraid I . . .'

'Well, it's this most lovely mansion in the Rue de Varenne, and it's simply stuffed full of his works. Most people's image of Rodin starts and ends with monumental sculpture like 'The Thinker', 'The Kiss', 'The Burghers of Calais' and the like. But, for me, Rodin is exemplified by a little terracotta head of a girl in a straw hat covered in flowers, which I guess most people pass by in the Musée Rodin. I'd stake that little girl against all the famous pictures of the Louvre any day. Does that make me a Philistine?'

'Not one scrap,' replied Fosdyke. 'I will record you in my survey as a 'Don't Know'. And in the light of your answer, the second question, which is 'What is the next most famous painting in the Louvre?' is somewhat irrelevant. Um— Miss . . . '

'Batthyány,' she prompted him.

'If you haven't lunched, would you care to take luncheon with me here? They do—um—all sorts of dishes as far as I can see.'

'Oh, Mr Fosdyke, I am so sorry,' she said, 'but I have a lunch appointment already, and already I am late. It's been so nice meeting you, and I'm most regretful that I've been no use at all in your survey.'

'Oh, you have, you have,' he assured her. 'The— um—negative comments are equally of value to our—ah— deliberations. And I may say that I shall go and see the little terracotta head of the girl in the straw hat at the earliest opportunity.'

'How nice,' she said, and, rising, held out her hand—her small and well-shaped hand. 'Goodbye, Mr Fosdyke. So nice to have met you. And thanks for the drink.'

'*Tomorrow!*' Fosdyke blurted out the word much louder than he needed, and a lot of people paused in mid-act of eating and drinking to stare at him with glowering resentment.

'Tomorrow?' repeated Miss Batthyány questioningly.

'Lunch with me tomorrow,' said Fosdyke. 'Here—at this time. Would you—please?'

'Well, yes, that would be nice,' she replied. 'Here, at this time. I shall look forward to that. Till then, au revoir.'

'Au revoir,' he replied, and watched her go out of the glass door and walk in the swirling snow down the Rue Royale in the direction of the Place de la Concorde. Still standing and gazing, and with most of the nearby drinkers and eaters staring at him in turn, a most disturbing thought struck him . . .

What, if by some means, she was unable to keep their date? She had no way of communicating with him, nor he with her. Fool!—he should have organized an exchange of addresses!

But it was still not too late . . .

He leapt for the door, and was out of it not one half a second before the waiter who had served them espied his intent.

'Monsieur—stop!—Votre addition! . . .'

Heedless of the fact that he had not yet settled his bill, his only thought to catch her before she was swallowed up—perhaps for ever . . . in the maelstrom of Paris, he disregarded the call, and ran down the street with the waiter (who was considerably older than he and, despite a lifetime of working on his feet and carrying heavy trays, by no means a fit man) very close upon his heels and giving forth mightily:

'Au voleur! Stop thief!'

She was out of sight! Had she turned right, as if up the Champs Elysées?

'Au secours! Au voleur! Cet homme-là—c'est un voleur!'

Or had she turned left, crossed the road (against the traffic, and at what peril to herself on the slippery road. Oh God, would he find her just round the corner, the centre of a gawping circle: a still form lying on the pavé, with an agent de police laying his cloak reverently over the worst of what had been so divinely lovely?).

'Assassin! Revolutionnaire!'

He skidded round the corner of the street and nearly fell. The act brought the pursuing waiter so close to him that he was able to secure a firm hand-hold on the collar of his coat, shouting the odds the meantime, and attracting the attention of an agent de police, who, relinquishing his duty for the time being in the interests of higher crime as opposed to the frivolity of assembling some order in the to-ings and fro-ings in the Place de la Concorde around the hour of luncheon, strolled across towards them—but in no great haste.

Bernard Fosdyke had no interest in all this; neither in the hand that held him, nor in the advancing presence of the Law; his whole attention was upon the slight, but shapely, figure of the young woman. He saw her pause as a sleek limousine, sounding its two-tone horn, called her attention and drew suavely in to the kerb. He divined that some sort of transaction was taking place between her and the driver, for she shook her head, but afterwards gave a shrug of acquiescence and got into the car, which drove away at some pace.

'Oh no,' he breathed. And then again: 'Oh no! Not that!'

Something of the tragedy in his demeanour must have communicated itself to the waiter and the policeman, for they ceased their excited cross-talk, their frenzied Gallic gesticulations; and two grave, compassionate pairs of eyes were directed towards the object of their former discourse, as he stood, bereft, pale and wrung-out, staring after the disappearing limousine.

'M'sieur . . .' The waiter's hand stole towards Fosdyke's arm and touched it gently. 'Are you perhaps not veree h-okay?'

Mute, Fosdyke took out his battered pocket book, extracted from it one of his fifty-franc notes, placed it in the other's hand, and walked slowly away.

'Une femme lui a tourné la tête.'

'Cherchez la femme, Jean,' responded the policeman, who was a friend of his, 'et on la trouve toujours.'

It could be said that the Authors' College débâcle greatly changed Bernard Fosdyke's view of life, though not to any advantage.

There afterwards followed a painful interview with his bank manager at which that worthy spelt out in no mean terms that the repayments of £15 monthly would have to be honoured, so Mr Fosdyke had better get himself some gainful employment; and good day to you, Mr Fosdyke, rising and extending a frigid hand.

At first, it seemed that there might still be something to salvage from the wreckage. He was still in contact with no less than thirty putative authors, who, following the inducement to match what they had in common with Kipling, Mark Twain, Edgar Wallace, et al, and having paid out good money for their course of instruction, were mostly quite keen to keep it up. Fosdyke burnt a lot of midnight oil in correcting their essays, incidentally learning a lot about writing while he taught—a by no means uncommon occurrence in any branch of the arts. He also began to write his first novel in what might laughably be called his 'spare time'.

Further to retain his 'customers', he prepared a cyclostyled letter to the chosen thirty, offering them what might loosely be described as a post-graduate course in advanced writing coupled with critical appreciation of the great masters of the art. Five guineas a time. He had one applicant only: a Mrs Edna Furbright of Weemsdale Cottage, Beach Road, Mablethorpe, Lincolnshire. And it was the furtherance of Mrs Furbright's career—a very demanding lady determined to succeed—that may be said to have brought Bernard Fosdyke to drink: the long nights spent in correcting her abysmal attempts to emulate the novels of V. Sackville-West and of Miss Edith Sitwell, together with other ladies of the current literary beau monde, so ravaged his mental and physical stamina as to bring him close to a complete breakdown which he avoided only by having printed a specious Certificate of Doctorate of Philosophy (Ph.D., Lit., Auth. Coll.), which he sent to Mrs Furbright and which she treasured and so styled herself as till the end of her days.

The Authors' College having petered out as a means of gainful occupation, and the gentle importunities of his bank manager becoming ever less gentle, Bernard Fosdyke then addressed himself to the labour market, which, considering the state of world economy and his own lack of experience or qualifications put him very near the end of the queue for jobs. However, there is a mode of livelihood, more like a drudgery, which is forever open to the brave and the strong, many of whom prosper: the occupation of door-to-door salesmen, not on salary or wages, but on commission upon results. Fosdyke applied for such a job, and, because he had the superficial requirements: one decent suit in which he presented himself for the place, a 'good' accent and—thanks to his exotic ancestry—a quite handsome and striking appearance, he was received into the Encyclopædia Universal Company as a trial and trainee sales representative on two and a half per cent commission—which meant that, if he managed to sell one set of the twelve volumes of the encyclopædia a week he would be able to meet the demands of the bank and also feed, board and clothe himself. Provided he didn't eat too often.

The dispensation of the Encyclopædia Universal, which was an American company with outlets in all English-speaking countries, centred, for the benefit of its native tongue, in Croydon, Surrey. There, daily, Bernard Fosdyke presented himself, and was particularly impressed by a fellow salesman of considerable repute in the sort of donkey-Derby that the Company floated, whereby the 'sales representative' who made the highest score in any twelvemonth got a five per cent bonus on top. The man in question, one Hesman, a man of pouchy eyes, could have sold lead weights to shipwrecked sailors.

In addition to being a mine of arcane information on the ins and outs of encyclopædia-selling ('If there's no kid in the house, you're wasting your time. Sell to the kid. Then work on its mum or its dad, whoever's wearing the trousers: suggest that neglecting to buy is going to destroy the little bugger's educational chances for life') he had also perfected the art of mixing business with pleasure to the extent of satisfying his very considerable romantic requirements while at work—or so he claimed. ('The state of the garden's the giveaway. Show me a house with an overgrown lawn and weeds climbing up the walls and I'll show you a home where the hubby spends all his nights round at the pub, and his wife sits at home dreaming of a white knight like Ronald Colman or Doug Fairbanks to come and carry her off. As soon as I see that unkempt garden, I say to myself, 'Get in there, Charlie-boy, you can't lose.''')

Now Bernard Fosdyke, at that time over thirty and should have known better, was still in the state that has delicately been described as celibacy unannealed. Much of the blame for this must be laid at the door of his confined upbringing as a quasi-invalid, a withdrawn and self-regarding person whose quite attractive looks were soured by a rather petulant mouth, and with a really quite buoyant spirit that tended to be tongue-tied when crossed to the slightest degree (in other words, he sulked a lot). Neither of these qualities greatly endeared him to members of the opposite sex, which was a constant source of puzzlement to Bernard, who, not unmindful of the superficial charms that he regarded in his shaving mirror every morning, could never understand how it was that other men: older men, fat, balding, common, vulgar, were able to attract nubile women. His lament could be encapsulated in the words of the popular song:

'If women like her like fellers like him,
Why don't women like me?'

It was a question which he had addressed to himself in the months of his encyclopædia-selling period, and had been no nearer an answer till the fateful lunchtime when he had met a perfect stranger in the Rue Royale, with snowflakes drifting all round them both like wedding confetti, and had seemed to find it almost within his grasp—only to have it snatched away most cruelly.

Harold Hiram Levy was already there at the Café des Deux Magots when Fosdyke arrived about a quarter of an hour late, shook the snow from his hat, took off his overcoat and sat down. The café was full to overflowing.

'How did you make out, Bernie?' asked the other. 'You look like you've just trudged your way back from the North Pole. I guess a drink wouldn't be entirely out of court.'

'Oh, please—yes,' responded Fosdyke.

The touch of Scotch on his palate was like the balm of mother's milk; its immediate effect upon his empty stomach to make him almost throw up. Levy watched him in silence.

'May I take it you've had a trying afternoon?' he asked.

'It started off—rather badly—but after that became merely routine,' said Fosdyke. 'Most interesting in a way. I don't know if the result confirms whatever preconceived notion you may have, but, if it does, it does so quite un-equivocally. Do you want to hear it now?'

'Tell,' said Levy.

Fosdyke produced his cheap notebook, to which he re-ferred. 'In answer to the first question,' he said, 'of the eighty-seven people I canvassed, fifty-five plumped for Leonardo da Vinci's *Mona Lisa*. Eleven for *The Virgin of the Rocks* by the same artist. Of the remainder, there were six single choices that varied in subject-matter from Géricault's *Raft of the Medusa* to various female nude subjects—the latter delivered to me with many winks, prods and nods. And fifteen didn't know. Or want to know.'

'Excellent,' was Levy's comment. 'And to the second question?'

'Well, that was very odd, because the folks who voted for *Mona Lisa* invariably went for *The Virgin of the Rocks* as their second. On the other hand, the rest simply didn't have any opinion at all worth a mention. The Don't Knows were as high as twenty-eight. In short, those whom you describe as The Man in the Street regard the Louvre museum for all practical purposes as a repository for the *Mona Lisa*. With *The Virgin of the Rocks* as a bad—a very bad—second.'

Levy rubbed his hands. 'Excellent!' he exclaimed. 'Quite excellent! Now, we'll go someplace for dinner. You look half-starved, Bernie. Put yourself entirely in my hands.'

Fosdyke regarded his companion with a certain watchfulness. 'And will you tell me what all this is about?' he quizzed. 'The survey of the Man in the Street, the fortune that's coming to us both. All that?'

'Sure,' replied Levy. 'I'll tell you all about it over dinner, never fear.'

Levy took him to a homely little restaurant that was only a hundred yards from the café: there were two rows of plain wooden-topped tables scrubbed to pristine whiteness and a smell of plain cuisine. The speciality of the establishment was tête de veau, visibly cooked by Madame, a lady of fairly advanced years wearing a kitchen apron and a watchful eye. Sizing up Levy and Fosdyke as foreigners, she bundled an elderly gentleman and his pile of books (addressing him as 'cher monsieur le professeur' as she did so) from what was obviously the only prestigious table for two on to one of the long, communal tables.

'Vin?' she addressed them when they were seated. And Levy assented.

The wine was the wine of the house and there was no

other. It was red, raw, and quite excellent. The stewed calves' cheek was likewise totally lacking in pretension and equally splendid. The two men ate in absorbed silence for a while. Up at the counter, Madame poured herself half a tall glass of the house wine, topped it up with water, took a long swig, pronounced it to be 'Très bon', belched, and went back to stirring the calves' cheek stew.

Presently Levy said: 'Bernie, as I have already observed, you carry the air of a man who has had a trying day, and by your continued manner of—shall we say tristesse?—you communicate to me that this is not entirely concerned with stomping the boulevards of Paris in a mild fall of snow. Do I have it right? Something happened to you since last we met. Correct?' The clever, shrewd eyes fixed his companion and Fosdyke knew that there was no escape in evasion.

'Yes,' he admitted.

'Tell uncle.'

'I—I . . .'

'Spit it out, nephew mine.'

'Well, I met this rather super girl. She was—quite different from any I've ever known. And I was quite—well—smitten.'

'So—hooray! This is a cause for celebration. Bring on the champagne and the dancing girls. Pray accept my hand in congratulation. But—ah!—there is a complication, perhaps. Tell on, nephew mine.'

'I met her during the survey,' confessed Fosdyke, and the confession, once begun, poured out of him in extreme heat, purging the dark humours that he had accumulated throughout the long afternoon and early evening since he had seen her . . . seen her . . .

'Yes? And there was an immediate chemical reaction between you, perhaps—it was mutual?'

'Oh yes,' replied Fosdyke with some vehemence, 'I sensed that very strongly. Particularly at the end, when we parted, and I felt emboldened to ask her to meet me at the same time and in the same place for luncheon tomorrow.'

Levy spread his hands and hunched his shoulders. 'My life, where is then your problem, Bernie?' he asked.

'Well . . .'

(Here the catharsis of the confessional became stuck. Should he say: Well, this goddess who walked into my life at one end, walked out of the other into the arms of some rich swine in a limousine who had to do no more than raise his price before she accepted his offer? As lief not have raised the subject at all.)

'Go on,' prompted Levy, attributing his companion's hesitation to an entirely different reason. 'So where's the problem? You meet this no doubt lovely girl tomorrow for lunch. You engage her in amorous dalliance and charm her right out of her mind. In due course, you either go back to your place, or you go back to her place.' He paused, suddenly taken by a concept, and eyed his companion even more closely.

After a while, having made sure that they were out of earshot of the other clientèle (the nearest was the professor, who was totally engaged in a book while forking tête de veau into his mouth in slovenly fashion, with the aid of a haunch of bread), Levy leaned forward and whispered:

'I think I discern your problem, Bernie. Are you perhaps a—?' He mouthed the word silently.

'Oh no—no!' retorted Fosdyke with some heat. 'I'm perfectly normal in every respect. Except—' he added for-lornly—'I might be said to be somewhat—*retarded* . . .'

'Oh, Bernie!' exclaimed Levy, and again he looked round to make sure no one should hear, lest shame be brought upon them both. 'You are telling me now, in this year of nineteen hundred and thirty-three, that you, who must be around the same age as this present century, are a—a—?' Again he mouthed the operative word.

Fosdyke nodded miserably.

Levy snapped his finger and thumb dismissively. 'No problem,' he declared, 'no problem at all. You will meet your little inamorata for luncheon tomorrow and you will disport yourself well in the lists of Hymen, if I may be excused the fanciful and classical allusion.

'As soon as we have finished dinner, Bernie (and I may say that I am calling for another helping of this tête de veau, which is not a dish, but a poem), I am taking you straight to a veritable temple of Hymen, where you will—in the arcane phrase of your British game of cricket—*break your duck*, and in a manner which will greatly illuminate the rest of your career in that area.

'But first, over our second helpings, Bernie, let us discuss the making of our joint fortunes . . .'

'As to what I am,' said Levy, later, 'I am a picture forger. Does that surprise you, Bernie? You don't draw away from me in distaste. This I attribute to your innate criminality of which I have spoken before, and which commended you to me in the first place.'

'You must find it—very profitable,' said Fosdyke, remembering the Rolls, the matched crocodile luggage, the bankroll so lightly borne.

'I do,' responded his companion. 'If I were an avant-garde painter, applauded as such by the likes of the phonies of the Deux Magots and their sort, I should undoubtedly be the highest paid painter in the world. As it is, I am by far the highest paid forger. Some time tomorrow, after we have amused ourselves this evening in the temple of Hymen, and either before or after you have met your petite amie, I may demonstrate my ability by knocking off a little Renoir before your very eyes, for which I already have a rich buyer in Amsterdam.'

'Astonishing!' declared Fosdyke, and took a deep draught of the heady red wine. 'But where do I come into all this, Hal? I mean, I have no artistic competence—save in the literary field,' he added modestly.

'Ah, your question brings me to the heart and centre of

my secret,' replied Levy. 'The business of simple art forgery
—such as the creation of a passably fine Rubens, a Daumier
cartoon, a boating scene by Renoir—pictures which the said
masters *might* have produced but never did—in other words,
mere pastiches—are the smallest part of my profit. What
you might call the bread-and-butter side of my operation,
the big money, the nascent fame, lies in my *re-creation* side.
Do you want to hear more?'

'But of course,' declared Fosdyke, fascinated.

'I am taking you greatly on trust,' said Levy. 'The business of my small frauds is of no very great moment. It is
what I am pleased to call my grand œuvre that could
likely land me in a whole peck of trouble if it came out
inopportunely.'

'I shall respect your confidence, Hal,' said Fosdyke.
'Upon my word as an Old Trumpingtonian,' he added,
invoking the name of the absurd little private school to
which his French nanny had hand-led him. 'What is the
nature of your grand œuvre?'

'I re-create the great painted masterpieces of the world,'
said Levy. 'Then, having taken the originals from the walls
of the principal national galleries, I replace them with my
own copies.'

Fosdyke, flatly disbelieving him, filled the gap of silence
by taking another swallow of wine.

'You don't believe me,' said Levy.

Fosdyke shrugged. 'I'm open to conviction,' he said. 'I
take it that my afternoon's efforts were directed towards
your supposition that the *Mona Lisa,* being the most popular
favourite picture in the Louvre, is the one most suitable for
your next operation of removal and replacement. Do I have
it right?'

Levy shook his head. 'No.'

'Oh, well. What then?'

Levy pointed his finger at his companion. And the Viking
eyes blazed with the lust of battle, plunder and rapine. 'I

sent you out to check my theory as to the *second most* popularly famous picture in one of the world's most prestigious galleries,' he said. 'You came back with the answer that I had predicted.' He laid his hand on Fosdyke's shoulder, leaning forward across the table to do so. 'Already well advanced in my Paris studio, I have painted a copy of *The Virgin of the Rocks*. Presently, and with your assistance, I shall ring the changes on the wall of the Louvre and you and I, my friend, will clean up a cool half-million each.'

Bemused, only half-believing, Fosdyke could simply only stare at his companion for quite a while—till the basic illogicality of the other's premise hit him hard.

He, too, pointed in his turn. 'But, like I've told you just now,' he declared, 'you're going after *second* best. My figures irrefutably prove that the *Mona Lisa* is by far the most famous picture in the Louvre. Indeed, in my opinion, she is arguably the most famous portrait in the whole wide world.'

Levy looked as smug as his Viking features would allow.

'Quite so,' he said. 'And would you not believe that the version of the said painting which is now viewed by gawping idolators by the thousand in the Louvre museum, is from the hand of yours sincerely Harold Hiram Levy?'

'You don't mean. . .' breathed Fosdyke, astounded.

Levy nodded. 'Feller, I rang the changes on the *Mona Lisa* in nineteen twenty-nine, having met up with a multi-millionaire oil tycoon while advising him on the building of a replica of the Vatican in Southern California as a love-nest to house his mistress, who was a torch singer of religious persuasion. He had that original Leonardo masterpiece for peanuts. I was new to the game in those days. *The Virgin of the Rocks* will cost him, as a companion piece to the *Mona Lisa* (though the term 'companion piece' is a misnomer, they being respectively sacred and profane in subject-matter, and also of a different scale), a million dollars. Which he will gladly pay. And together they will hang in the selfsame boudoir in that selfsame Vatican replica, and be admired for their snob appeal and their intrinsic worth by his mistress. Not, I would add, by the *same* mistress; the torch singer has long been replaced at many removes by an ex-42nd Street stripper.

'Money, Bernie, is a great leveller. It cuts through the irrelevant flim-flam of generic stupidity and induced semi-illiteracy, allowing us to appreciate the best things in life for what they're really worth. And it's not a lot.

'Or has this fine raw wine, coupled with the weight of tête de veau that I have consumed, somewhat over-stimulated the gentle cynicism that lies close to the heart of every artist?'

CHAPTER 4

Levy paid their bill (it was not cheap), and drove to the place that he persisted in calling 'a temple of Hymen' or une maison de rendezvous—but never a brothel.

Fosdyke's view of the current enterprise was clouded by the admixture of grape and grain which, to him, was unaccustomed and had not made a good chemical combination in his brain or in his stomach; furthermore, though he basically dreaded the proposition of visiting a brothel to 'break his duck', he did not feel his position strong enough, in relation to his new friend/mentor/benefactor/partner, to argue the point.

While he was speculating on all this, his companion was expanding upon their forthcoming art fraud, with particular regard to the financial share-out.

'A million,' he said. 'A million has a kind of finite elegance. Know what I mean? Split two ways. That suit you?'

'I think it's more than generous of you, Hal,' responded Fosdyke. 'But I don't see how I can possibly earn an equal part of the sum in question. I mean—you are the chap with the expertise, you are painting the replacement picture which, upon your own admission, will possibly fool the art experts till the end of time. Whereas what role shall I play? That of conducting a survey in the streets of Paris? You may have in mind that I drive the getaway car; I have to tell you that I can't drive. As to adding one cubit to the picture's worth—Hal, I can't even draw a straight line.'

'You *have* what you *have*, Bernie,' said the other, and hiccuped.

'Oh, you'll have to do better than that,' protested Fosdyke. 'Particularize, I beg you. *Particularize!*'

'Like I explained you before,' said Levy, 'you have fundamentally a criminal mind, the essential of which—be the guy in question a practising criminal or no—is a subtle and guileful imagination. Now, though I am engaged upon what the world would call "criminal pursuits", I do not possess this quality. What I possess—along with the arty phonies of the Café des Deux Magots—is the characteristic of the Complete Artist: I will do anything for money. But I don't have the guileful imagination to bring my creativity to pecuniary fruition. You, I'm convinced, have this quality —along with your predecessor, my late friend Mr Nathan T. Willis, sometime of Hoboken, New Jersey.'

'You formerly had another partner?' exclaimed Fosdyke. 'Ah, that would seem to explain the motive behind your interest in what you suppose to be my proclivities. Mr Willis had the same, you say?'

'Yes, indeed.'

'He—perhaps—assisted you in the switch of the *Mona Lisa*?'

'Yes.'

'Devised the means by which the switch could be made, perhaps?'

'Yes.' Levy's eyes, lit up by the flickering, passing lights of the boulevard, grew dreamy with nostalgia. 'I left the whole thing—the plan for the switch—entirely to Nathan.

What he came up with was an idea so simple, so pristine; with all the charm and innocence and totally surreal un-expectedness of a young child picking daisies within yards of the front line trenches in the Great War. It was exquisite. Masterly. Like a soufflé done to perfection.'

'Do tell,' said Fosdyke, intrigued and amused, as well he might have been.

So Levy began.

They turned down the Boulevard St Germain, heading for the Concorde bridge, and all Paris was alight with the tiny droplets of sleet that fell into the great canyons of the streets and reflected the headlamps, the street lamps, the glow from the shop windows.

'I met Nathan Willis right here in Paris in the spring of 'twenty-nine,' said Levy. 'He was a student of engineering in some Mid-Western college and over here on vacation of a rather extended kind—he'd been slung out of college for embezzling fraternity house social funds, as he later confessed to me with no shame.

'I first overheard him in some café persuading some gullible old American visitor that he was an ex-professional baseball player who had had to quit through an injury to his spine and was starving here in Paris. It was beautifully done. When the old guy had handed over a ten-dollar bill and left, Nathan met my eye and grinned. I challenged him to tell who'd won the World Series the previous year, but he just laughed. He neither knew nor cared.

'We had some drinks together—and he told me all about himself and how he was making out in Paris by drifting around and picking up a few dollars here and a few francs there. But what intrigued me was the sheer diversity of his ideas. From what I've learned, these kinds of feller are usually pretty dumb. Unless they're in the top class, they stick with one trick, one spiel, two at the most, and inevitably get caught. Now Nathan, he had a trick for every situation, a dozen times a day.

'It was then I knew that fickle Fate had brought us together.'

The Rolls bowled over the bridge, and the Seine and the swirling sleet met in murky whiteness far below. Fosdyke shivered and drew himself closer into his warm coat.

'You already had the notion to switch the *Mona Lisa?*' he asked. 'And I suppose, consciously or subconsciously, you were looking out for a Nathan T. Willis?'

Levy nodded in the loom of passing lights. 'It happened like this,' he said. 'The painting came first. Already, I'd been making a good living on the side with my pastiches of Degas, Renoir and the rest. I did the copy of the *Mona Lisa* as a challenge to myself, to the notion of my own brilliance. I even showed it to the millionaire guy with the replica Vatican when he came over to Paris. He it was who came up with this wild idea to make the switch, and offered me fifty thousand dollars if I could deliver the original Leonardo and successfully have my copy accepted in its place on the wall.

'Bernie, you wouldn't believe how the very notion of it sent the adrenalin rushing through my veins like absolute alcohol. The concept of having the walls of the great galleries of Europe and America hung with the works of Harold Hiram Levy and revered as world masterpieces had me (and I say it with my hand on my heart) punch-drunk with emotion for all of three days. For I looked ahead, you see, Bernie. I figured that if it could be done with the Leonardo, it could be done with a dozen others—*if only I knew how to work the switch!*

As they rounded the classical bulk of the Madeleine, and Fosdyke was still casting a yearning backward glance to the café where he had so coyly importuned Dorothy Batthyány (but not to think of that, not that!) it seemed to him that his companion's declaration called for comment.

'Despite your assertion, my dear Hal, that you as an artist would do anything for money, I think there is n ore to it from your point of view. In what you call your grand œuvre, there is a hidden compulsion.'

'As usual, you search me out and find me, Bernie. The compulsion, as you call it, is to cock a snook at the *avant garde* of the European and American art world, as exemplified by the sleek cats of the Deux Magots back there, who dismiss me as an artist simply because I can draw and paint in the grand manner which they consider to be irrelevant to this day and age.'

'But they must still hold such as Leonardo in high regard,' said Fosdyke. 'They'd be laughed to scorn if they didn't.'

'Of course they do,' retorted Levy. 'But Leonardo and his like present no competition to them. He is safely dead. Better than that, he and his like, their works lying back there in the Louvre, can conveniently be accorded the sort of pious regard with which one occasionally recalls dear little Jo-Jo, Fido, or whatever—now safely interred in the cute dogs' cemetery on that island in the Seine.

'Only—and here's the cream of the jest—they are already paying lip service to Harold Hiram Levy—*and all unknowing!*'

This declaration seemed to drain Fosdyke's companion of his energy, for he was silent for a while, and brought a hip flask to his lips a couple of times, first offering it to Fosdyke, who declined.

By this time, Levy had driven away from the main streets, and the Rolls was passing between narrow, high-walled blocks of apartment houses that must surely have pre-dated Baron Haussmann's rebuilding of Paris in the 1860s, and from whose dark entrances one might have expected to come reeling the drunken Danton or the primly mincing Robespierre.

'Nearly there,' said Levy. 'You're going to love this place.'

'To continue your story,' prompted Fosdyke. 'I take it

that, with his expertise, Willis speedily devised the means of working the switch?'

'That he did,' responded the other. 'Within two days, I was able to cable the Big Man in Southern California and tell him that I was ready to proceed. When he had my wire, he sent over one of his trusted aides—the sort of guy who would frisk his mother's corpse before they laid it in the coffin, for fear that she had concealed in her grave-clothes the family's silver spoons. This guy came over and monitored the switch, to make sure that his boss got the real goods and not H. H. Levy's copy.'

'And it was so done—the Big Man got the original Leonardo?'

'He did.'

'And *how* was the switch made, Hal? I can't wait to hear.'

'The next instalment of my saga will have to wait awhiles, Bernie-boy, for we have arrived at the temple of the spoilt Vestals. But, if we get a few minutes to ourselves during the next few hours remaining of this wakeful night—which I doubt—I will enlighten you.'

He brought the Rolls to a halt by a dark doorway of a shuttered house in a quiet, high-walled street.

Paris in those dear, dead days of 1933 contained more maisons de rendezvous—that is to say, properly licensed establishments, as opposed to the specialist hotels in the back streets—than stand record today; the records having been expunged when the saintly Marthe Richard of the Paris Municipal Council proposed and had carried a motion to close down these dens of iniquity and female degradation —as a result of which the girls were deprived of the pampered role of birds in gilded cages and had to take to the streets, or to make shift with the kind of ad hoc hotel arrangements which Bernard Fosdyke had unwillingly witnessed on his first night in the capital. Some traces of the most famous and de luxe of the maisons de rendezvous

remain in the folk memory of the faithful: Le Sphinx and
Le One-One-Two spring most readily to mind—as also
does a more modest, neighbourhood establishment called
La Ronde, to whose door Fosdyke and Levy, bowing their
heads against the sleet, made a concerted dive on the night
in question.

Business was not good, that night, at La Ronde, for there is
little to quench the ardour of the male like the prospect of
turning out into the wintry, windy darkness, when the
café across the street beckons with the promise of male
companionship; even staying at home with a good bottle of
wine, a bit of music on the t.s.f., comfortable slippers and
the wife, is not without merit.

Mme Brunelleschi and the girls had resigned themselves
to a quiet night. Madame had taken off her stays and put
her feet up; the girls had put on woolly cardigans over their
long dresses of art silk and crêpe-de-chine and were playing
faro or solitaire; Loulou the doorman in his Arabian slave
get-up was lolling against the gate of the glass-panelled and
gilded lift and limning his fingernails with swift, sure strokes
of carmine; behind the bar, Jules the bartender was slumped
with his elbows on the counter, gazing through the smoke
of the cigarette that dangled from his lips and fantasizing
about summer afternoons on the beach at Trouville, with
the slender figures of boys in bathing costumes wavering in
the heat-haze as they strolled languorously down towards
the glassy sea.

Then came the knock on the door.

'Attention au commerce!' cried Mme Brunelleschi.

Such activity followed! Like an overturned apiary, the
establishment came seethingly alive. Loulou made a dive
for the door, pausing for a moment and looking round to
see if all was in readiness to receive the business, one hand
on the slide of the Judas window. He had not long to wait.
In a trice, Madame had done up her stays, the woolly

cardigans were out of sight, Jules had doused his cigarette, straightened himself up, pressed the bell to the kitchen to warn Florence the cook to heat up the bouillon. Fixed smiles everywhere.

Loulou slid open the Judas window; perceived an anxious face, a hat bedecked with glistening pinpoints of sleet. It was a good face, a reasonably sober face moreover. He opened the door to Levy and Fosdyke.

'Bonsoir, messieurs.' Then, his practised eye summing them up, he switched to English: 'Welcome to La Ronde.'

Mme Brunelleschi evaluated her guests: with one long upward and downward sweep of her heavily-lashed eyes she had their quality and station, priced their clothes, determined how drunk they were or how sober. Satisfied, she extended a regal hand.

'Good evening, gentlemens,' she purred. 'Come and meet the girls. Jules—champagne!'

A cork popped. Two. And a tray of brimming glasses appeared as soon as Levy and Fosdyke had divested themselves of hats and overcoats for Loulou to bear away.

Fosdyke accepted a glass, and found himself looking over the rim of it into the laughing eyes of a little blonde with a turned-up nose.

'What ees your name?' she asked.

'Um—Bernard,' he responded.

'Is a nice name. I call you Bernard. I am Yvonne.'

'Um—hello, Yvonne.' Overcome with her proximity, by the heady intensity of their discourse, Fosdyke addressed himself to the champagne; but he could not stay submerged for ever; presently he had to surface. And she was waiting for him.

'You like to come upstairs with Yvonne?' she asked.

'I . . .' He glanced in wild desperation for a reassuring look, a supporting word, from his companion. Levy was chatting gaily to a redhead, one arm about her waist. He turned and winked at Fosdyke.

'Off with you and break your duck,' he said.

'What is thees duck, Bernard?' asked Yvonne.

'Well, it's—um—a cricketing term,' replied Fosdyke. 'Are you familiar with the British national game—er— Yvonne?'

Puzzled, she frowned and shook her blonde head.

'Well,' said Fosdyke, brightening, as he saw the light of salvation at the end of a tunnel, 'come and sit down here—' indicating a sofa, and registering that it was a good, wide sofa—'and I'll tell you all about cricket.'

Wonderingly, but good-natured still, she followed and sat down close beside Fosdyke, who had established himself in the middle of the sofa. No sooner had she done so than he slid to the opposite end. A cordon sanitaire now blessedly lay between them.

'Ah—cricket . . .' began Fosdyke, racking his brain.

'You don' like me, Bernard?' she asked, pouting.

'Why, of course I do—er—Yvonne,' he assured her fervently. (Too fervently, perhaps?) 'I think you're a simply super girl, I really do. But, as I was saying . . .'

'Then we go upstairs?'

'The origins of the game derive, as I recall, from the middle of the thirteenth century. The name itself is a corruption of the Old English word "cryce", meaning a stick . . .'

'I tell Jules to take a bottle of champagne up to my room, eh?'

'Yes, by all means—but no hurry, no hurry. The—er— game is played by two opposing teams of eleven men. Or eleven women. Or eleven girls. Or boys. Haha! . . .'

'The bottle of champagne is costing fifty francs.'

'Very reasonable prices here. The object of the game is to . . .'

'And two hundred francs for—you know.'

'Oh dear . . .'

'You pay madame now, eh?'

'The game has inspired some really quite notable verse,'

said he, his voice rising to a high pitch of desperation. 'One calls to mind:

> 'There's a breathless hush in the close tonight,
> Ten to make and the match to win—
> A bumping pitch and a blinding light . . .

'Aaaaaah!'

He cried out aloud—as, reaching, she laid a hand on his knee.

'You pay madame and we go upstairs, Bernard.' There was a slight but discernible edge to her voice now. Impatience? Menace, perhaps?

'Yes!' he cried. 'All right—I'll come!'

Then there was a knock at the street door.

All conversation ceased. All eyes were upon Loulou as he flew to the Judas window and pulled it aside.

Almost immediately, he closed it and turned to face Mme Brunelleschi, wild-eyed.

'Gaspardo!' he breathed.

'*Gaspardo!*' Yvonne echoed the name along with the others. Her hand fell limply from Fosdyke's knee.

In answer to another, more peremptory, knock, Loulou opened up and stood aside.

There were two of them. The leader—and, despite his small size and the monstrous bulk of his companion, there was leadership written all over him—was wearing an expensive camelhair coat with a wraparound-and-tie belt, a jaunty hat, neat pointed-toed shoes of the sort described as co-respondent's. The removal of the hat revealed patent leather brilliantined black hair that went with a swarthy countenance and button-black eyes. He took a cigar from his moist pink mouth and leered at the proprietress.

'Bonsoir, madame.'

'Bonsoir, m'sieu,' responded Mme Brunelleschi, and

seemed to shrink inside her stout stays and the black bomba-
zine evening frock that she wore.

The ensuing exchange, which was carried out in the rapid,
slurred vernacular of the St Antoine district, was just—
but only just, and imperfectly—within the competence of
Fosdyke's nursery French; it was just beyond that of Levy.
However, the manner of delivery, the menace on the one
hand and the fear on the other, rendered a clear understanding of the words scarcely necessary.

'First, you and I will do a little business, I think,
madame,' said the small man, who must be Gaspardo.
Contingent upon which, Mme Brunelleschi swallowed
hard, turned and walked through an archway leading into
a back room. With a wink towards his companion,
Gaspardo followed her.

The big man remained. Like his leader, he was expen-
sively if flashily dressed, and his massive form seemed
scarcely able to be contained by the suave tailoring. He
stood with arms folded; pale, piggy eyes creeping from one
to the other of the shrinking girls like encroaching larvae.
His gaze lit upon Levy and he scowled.

'Think you're pretty tough, I guess,' he growled.

Levy shrugged.

'I was in the Foreign Legion,' said the big man. 'Twelve
years. Morocco. Indo-China. Cameroons. I was a sergeant.'
He struck his massive chest. 'No fellow got tough with
Sergeant Delon. Once I killed a man with one blow.'

'Interesting,' said Levy.

This promising exchange was terminated by the return
of Madame and Gaspardo. She looked as if she had been
crying and there was a red weal across her cheek.
Pleasurably smirking, he was tucking something into his
breast pocket.

'And now, after the business—the girls!' he declared.

There was a discernible falling-off, a backing away,
among the girls. Yvonne, who was still seated next to

Fosdyke, stifled a gasp of alarm by pressing the back of her hand against her mouth.

Gaspardo went down the line of frightened females, till he came to a tall, statuesque brunette, whose eyes widened in terror.

'I'll take Solange,' he leered holding out his hand and seizing her wrist. 'Help yourself, Delon. Take two if you like. As always, it's all on the house.'

In the event, the former Foreign Legion sergeant was content with one girl. Her name was declared to be Marie, and her reaction to the big man's choice was much the same as that of her consœur. The foursome went towards the lift after the manner of slaughterers leading lambs to the abattoir. Loulou, pale-faced, opened the gates for them. They ascended out of sight.

'Mon Dieu!' breathed Yvonne, and crossed herself. 'Poor Solange. Poor Marie.'

'Who are those fellows?' asked Fosdyke.

She was not to be drawn, but merely shook her head and murmured something like 'very bad mens'.

The party atmosphere that existed before the arrival of Gaspardo and Delon might never have been. Woolly cardigans put in an appearance again and were wrapped around slender shoulders. The girls huddled together on chairs and sofas, two and three in a group, sad-faced, silent and still, like a tribe of capuchin monkeys.

'Suddenly this affair has turned into a wake,' murmured Levy. 'What say we bow out and go someplace else? You sure as hell aren't going to break your duck here tonight, Bernie.'

Fosdyke nodded, his spirits suddenly released.

'Oh, do not leave us!' pleaded Yvonne, who discerned their intent. 'Not until *they* have gone.' And her entreaty was echoed by the other girls.

Levy shrugged. 'I guess there's nothing else for it, Bernie,' he said.

'I suppose not,' assented the other, and he sat down again.

Yvonne wiped away a tear and shyly smiled at him.

'Do you play cards, Bernard?' she asked.

'A little,' he replied. 'But only whist.'

'I will get the cards.'

And so, by chance, he was safe.

But no . . .

'When they have gone,' she said, dealing the cards with devastating expertise, 'we will go upstairs.'

Half an hour later—and Yvonne was leading by seven games to two—the whirr of the descending lift signalled the return of the intruders who had turned a quiet evening at La Ronde into a nightmare. They were alone. Gaspardo leading, they swaggered across to where Loulou was already waiting with their hats and overcoats in hopeful expectation of their immediate departure. Nor was he disappointed. There was a discernible lightening of the atmosphere as the two men shrugged themselves into their coats and put on their hats.

Loulou was already waiting to open the street door.

Gaspardo looked about him and leered.

'Bonsoir, mesdames et messieurs,' he purred.

Delon scowled across at Levy.

Loulou swung open the door, to admit a swirling cloud of enormous snowflakes. The two men went out into the darkness. The door closed.

Mme Brunelleschi fell back into an easy chair.

'Jules!'

'Madame?'

'Champagne and brandy mixed. For all. On the house.'

Levy grinned at Fosdyke. 'Looks like you're going to break your . . .'

'Hey!—What was that?'

'It—it sounded rather like a couple of motor-car tyres

blowing out,' supplied Fosdyke. 'But rather quietly. Muffled, as it were.'

'*The Rolls!*' cried Levy, stricken.

He raced for the door and wrenched it open, with his companion at his heels. Outside was like some outer purlieu of the North Pole; one almost expected to see a dog-sled come slithering through the thick whiteness. And the descending snow quite blanked out the other side of the street. The Rolls retained nothing but its bulk, all its beauty of line hidden beneath the concealing blanket of white.

Everything was white. Except for two figures that lay, face downwards, side by side, and close beside the Rolls. And already the snow was beginning to cover them up.

'Holy cow!' said Levy. 'It's—*them!*'

By the light from the open door of the bordello, where the watching women were clustered, they turned over the smaller of the two figures. Gaspardo stared sightlessly up at them, mouth open as if to exclaim, an expression of mild surprise on his suddenly vulnerable face.

'He's dead!' said Levy. 'This guy is croaked!'

'Il est mort—Oh mon Dieu!' from the doorway.

· 'So's this one,' said Fosdyke, and seeing a tiny dab of pinkness marring the sheer white of the newly-fallen snow between the giant's shoulder-blades, he investigated closer. 'Great Scott, there's a small hole in the back of his coat!'

Their eyes met.

'He's been shot—they've both been shot!'

CHAPTER 5

From a sense of delicacy, Fosdyke and Levy dragged the two bodies inside the house—and with no help from Loulou and Jules, who shrank away along with the womenfolk. The door was shut. With the same sense of delicacy, Fosdyke covered the two dead faces with their own hats.

'We'd best call the cops, Bernie,' said Levy.

'Sure. I'll do that right away.' And, turning: 'Whereabouts is the phone, madame?'

'No, no!' The woman's reaction was immediate, horrified, and quite unequivocal. 'You cannot do this thing. You must take them away from here. Immédiatement! If they are found anywhere near La Ronde, I am finished. We are all finished!'

Fosdyke breathed heavily and counted up to three before he replied, and when he did so it was with the gentle patience of a man addressing himself to explaining red to a blind man: 'Madame, what you ask is impossible,' he said.

'That's right,' confirmed Levy. 'Lady, you must be nuts.'

'The phone, madame,' repeated Fosdyke.

It was now Mme Brunelleschi's turn to be sweetly reasonable, a change of approach which she achieved with some effect. Her sternly intransigent expression softened and was pensive, putting one in mind of Whistler's painting of his mother.

'Listen to me, gentlemens,' she said quietly. 'These mens—' pointing to the two corpses lying side by side like effigies—'these mens was very bad mens, but with many friends. If they are found near La Ronde, we all suffer.'

'Bernard, Bernard!' Yvonne took his hand and gazed up into his eyes. She really was a pretty little thing. 'Please help us, Bernard.'

The other girls added their entreaties.

'Nothing doing!' said Levy. 'Bernie, if we don't call the cops right away, we're in this thing up to our ears. Get to that phone!'

'NO!' Mme Brunelleschi barred Fosdyke's way. Now she was all virago. Liberty at the barricades. 'You will destroy yourselves if you do this thing!'

'Boloney!' said Levy.

'You do not know what you are doing!'

'We know well enough. Bernie—the phone.'

'The friends of these bad mens are powerful!'

'So are the cops.'

'They will know that you were here tonight if you tell the police.'

'They've got nothing on us—we're innocent.'

'These mens think nothing of innocence—only *vengeance*!'

'Oh!' exclaimed Fosdyke, and he looked to his companion for guidance. Levy said nothing.

'They will seek you out—they will find you!'

Still Levy said nothing.

'You will join—*them*!' She pointed to the two corpses.

Levy rubbed his chin. 'Madame,' he said, 'I think my friend and I are beginning to discern the subtle undertones of your argument.'

'Then—you will help us?'

'Um—just what do you have in mind?'

'Yes, what do you want us to do?' asked Fosdyke, who fully shared his companion's eminently sensible change of stance.

She told them.

Past one o'clock in the morning.

No one about, not even a patrolling police car. No one, save the roisterers still gathered in smoke-filled cabarets and nightclubs, was awake in the vicinity of the Champs Elysées, surely. Through his rear-view mirror, Levy saw the rear red lamp of a single car wind its way up the hill in the far distance towards the Arc de Triomphe.

'Over there, Hal,' said Fosdyke, pointing. 'That park bench.'

'Right!'

At the Concorde end of the great avenue, by the wooded park with the bandstands and cafés deserted under the snow, he switched off his lights and engine and let the Rolls glide up the pavement and on to the grass. A park bench described its shape under a counterpane of whiteness.

They lifted the two bodies out of the back, where they had lain together, one on top of the other like a pair of sardines in a tin. One by one, they carried them over to the bench and laid them down upon it on end, foot to foot.

There was a trash bin nearby. An idea striking Fosdyke, he delved inside and brought out a copy of *Le Figaro,* opened out the sheets of newsprint and laid them over the two corpses, faces and all. He then stood back and admired his handiwork.

'Good thinking,' said his companion. 'They'll be mistaken for a couple of hoboes sleeping rough, and won't be disturbed till morning—not unless a pushy cop happens along. Let's go, Bernie.'

'It seems rather hard to leave them without any obsequies,' said Fosdyke, lingering. 'At least we should have a Foreign Legion bugler to play The Last Post for ex-Sergeant Delon.'

'Let's not get maudlin at this stage,' growled Levy.

They crossed the Concorde bridge.

'We did the right thing, mind,' said Levy. 'The last thing we want right now is to get mixed up with the cops, let alone be piggies-in-the-middle in some gang war. My, but the madame of that whorehouse certainly has a persuasive tongue.'

'I was amused at the way she dived into Gaspardo's pocket and brought out that sheaf of banknotes that he'd presumably demanded from her for protection money.'

'That dame didn't rise to her present eminence by omitting to distinguish between the essentials and the non-essentials,' opined Levy. 'When it comes to looking after the last penny, I would back an average Parisian madame against any shark money-lender you'd care to produce. By the way, Bernie, I had in mind to take you back to my studio, show you a few things, and continue our discourse, but it's been a long day and two long nights.'

'I'm absolutely washed out,' confessed Fosdyke.

'I'll pick you up around ten o'clock,' said Levy. 'We'll have a late breakfast at the Deux Magots and I'll tell you the means by which the late genius Nathan T. Willis devised the switch with the *Mona Lisa*—the which feat you, with your essentially criminal mind, are shortly going to emulate.'

'You do me more than justice, Hal,' said Fosdyke. 'I hope I can match your high opinion of my abilities. I wonder— wouldn't it be possible to use the same method to switch the *Virgin?*'

Levy slowed down to take the corner leading to his companion's hotel.

'No on two counts,' he said. 'One—the very method, if employed a second time, would not only lead to certain failure in the case of the *Virgin,* but would compromise the replacement *Mona Lisa.* And, two—there is another factor (which I will show you tomorrow) which puts Nat Willis's scheme right out of court in this case.

'And here we are at your door. Gawd! Just look at those poor whores plying for trade at this hour, and in these conditions.'

In the shadow of the doorway were huddled two figures. Two pairs of eyes were directed towards the Rolls as it glided to a halt. It was to be supposed that in those eyes there was tremulous hope teetering on the edge of disbelief.

'Sleep well,' said Levy, as the other got out of the car. 'Pity you didn't break your duck before you meet your little *amie* for lunch tomorrow.' He grinned. 'But you still have a last chance tonight.' He nodded towards the two drabs in the doorway.

'Thanks for nothing, kind sir,' said Fosdyke. 'See you in the morning.'

As he reached to open the hotel door and enter the dingy hallway, a hand was laid upon his arm.

' 'Allo, chéri. Voulez-vouz . . .?'

'Non, merci, mam'selle,' responded Fosdyke rather brusquely. And then, as the light caught her face, he saw that she was old enough to have been his mother, and ill-worn and ill-used with it. Upon an impulse, he tugged out his wallet, extracted one of his fifty-franc notes and thrust it into her hand. He left her speechless.

Alone in the narrow bed in the narrow room, he lay for a while and watched the flashing lights of passing cars sweep across the ceiling above his head. It had been some night! It had been two nights and the best part of two days, beginning with the incident in Berlin!

He wondered if they had found the two bodies yet, and if he and Levy ran any risk, either from the police or from the murdered men's ubiquitous 'friends', of being implicated in the killings.

Drowsily, inconsequentially, he wondered how Hitler was enjoying his second night as Reich Chancellor of Germany, and rather hoped he wasn't.

In the end, having skirted the issue for so long, he asked himself if he was really going to keep the luncheon date with Dorothy Batthyány, and if indeed she would turn up; furthermore, if they both turned up, how would he be able to resist probing her about the pick-up he had witnessed, and how was he obliquely to broach the matter?

And supposing she lied to him? Or even supposing she was brutally frank about the whole thing . . .?

He was nagging his brain with this last question when he drifted into a quiet sleep.

At half past one in the morning, Commissaire Orlando Sanson and his wife were still rowing, as they had been continuously since half way through the expensive dinner that had been her birthday treat.

And then the phone rang in the downstairs hall. He let it ring for a while, because if it was someone from Head-quarters they would stay with it, knowing that his wife refused to allow a phone in the bedroom. And while he waited to learn if it was the real thing, or just some drunk with the wrong number, his wife kept up her peroration:

'I always knew you were no good! Right from our wedding, when you disappeared right after the meal, and didn't it just so happen—surprise!—that that slut Margot Lestrade went missing too!'

'You do go on about that,' he said wearily. 'And after all these years. I never laid a finger on Margot Lestrade in my life.'

'Oh no? Then why did you have lipstick on your collar when you condescended to return?'

'It was your lipstick,' he said. 'Now I've got to go and answer the phone.' He got out of bed, stepped into his slippers and pulled on his dressing-gown.

His wife's voice followed him out of the door, which he imperfectly closed, so that it swung open again when he was half way down the stairs.

'Liar! I wore "Rose Desire" lipstick. You came back with that vulgar "Blush Crimson"—HERS!'

He picked up the earpiece. 'Sanson here.'

'Commissaire, it's Dupuis.'

'What the hell—at this hour, Dupuis!'

'And there was that woman in—where was it?—St Malo. The one who left her hairpins scattered all over the back seat!'

'Sorry, Dupuis, will you say that again? We've got a bad connection.'

'I said we've got a double killing.'

'So? Can't you handle this till morning?'

'Certainly, Commissaire, but I thought you should know that . . . '

'You talked your way out of the woman in St Malo, but you didn't fool me, Orlando Sanson! Oh no!'

'WILL YOU SHUT UP! No, not you, Dupuis. Will you repeat that? I missed the last bit.'

'I said that the murdered men are two of our fellows—Inspector Gaspardo and Officer Delon.'

At nine o'clock the following morning, a silvery tri-engined civil airliner of Deutsche Lufthansa landed at Paris aerodrome and disgorged, among its other passengers, a man of distinctly military appearance. Tall and slender as an aspen, straight-backed, his figure offset by a black broadcloth coat that fitted him like a tube as far as the lower calf, he paused for a moment on the top step, careless of the people he held up behind him, and flashed a glance towards the aerodrome buildings as if looking for someone. There was icy authority in the glance and in the ascetic countenance, and iron command in the pale blue eyes, the left one of which gazed out through a rimless monocle that scorned any safety attachment to a ribbon. The set of the shaven head was haughty, yet with a touch of jauntiness of the military kind, underscored by the black fedora hat worn at a sharp angle over one ear. He carried a silver-knobbed cane and a briefcase, and his right cheek was deeply scored by a duelling scar.

'There he is—the Rittmeister!' From the wide windows of the reception building, the two men looked out and saw the newcomer at the top of the steps set against the airliner.

They went out to greet him. Both were identically dressed in black leather overcoats belted at the waist, pork-pie hats, mittened hands, big boots. Both were large men, cropped-headed, scowling. One was distinguishable from the other by reason of a toothbrush moustache and rimless spectacles.

They approached the aeroplane and the straggling line of passengers coming towards them. He whom they called the Rittmeister had slowed his pace till he was the last in line. When they came face to face with him, they halted in unison, clicked their heels, and—

'Heil Hit—'

'Not here, you fools!' The thin mouth bared in a snarl,

revealing gold-filled teeth. The right, unglazed eye flared with fury, while its neighbour remained immobile, retaining the monocle in place as if it had been screwed there. 'This is a confidential mission. It is important that we maintain a certain—discretion. Understood?'

Yes, they understood.

'We will go somewhere discreet and I will hear your report.'

'There is the car, Herr Rittmeister. Over there.'

'Excellent. Lead the way.'

A black limousine was parked behind the building. The monocled autocrat took his place in the precise centre of the rear passenger seat and motioned to the others to enter. They took their places on the two tip-up seats facing him; watched in awed silence as, taking from his breast pocket a crested and monogrammed silver case, he extracted a fat Egyptian cigarette and placed it in the end of an ivory holder.

Two mittened hands came out as one, each holding a lighter. Flick—flick—two tiny blossoms of flame were offered to him.

'Thank you,' he responded with a repellent civility. 'And now—your report!'

The two looked at each other. He of the moustache and spectacles nodded to his companion. It was the latter who commenced the narrative.

'Herr Rittmeister, following upon instructions, we drove at top speed to Cologne and the frontier. There they confirmed the response that they had made to inquiries at all frontiers. The silver Rolls-Royce passed through an hour previously. And the driver was—our man . . .'

'Yes, yes, I had all this when you telephoned last evening,' interposed the autocrat. 'What next? You located the subject, yes?'

'Yes, Herr Rittmeister, together with his companion.' He of the moustache and spectacles took up the narrative.

'Upon your order, we kept watch on the café in the Boulevard St-Germain where he first made contact with the agent acting for the Herr . . .'

'No names! No names—particularly not *his*!' blazed the other with such fury that his monocle remained in place by nothing short of a miracle. 'And then?'

'The subject arrived at the café and was shortly joined by a companion—presumably the accomplice who travelled into France with him. Later, they moved to a nearby restaurant, and afterwards drove to a house in the tenth district which, upon inquiry, we found to be a brothel . . .'

'We waited,' said his companion. 'An hour and a half later, they came out together . . .'

'And, as they reached out to touch the Rolls-Royce . . .'

'We shot them both in the back at long range . . . '

'With silenced pistols.'

'Dead—both?' snapped their interrogator. 'You examined the bodies, hein?'

'There was no need, Herr Rittmeister . . .'

'In the middle of the back, both. We never miss.'

'Excellent—excellent!' The autocrat smiled for the first time, and it was not a pleasant sight; putting one in mind of a poisonous snake which, having patiently watched a small furry victim die in agony, now bares its fangs to devour it whole.

The two subordinates beamed with pleasure, and he of the spectacles felt constrained to take them off and polish away the mistiness caused by his high emotion.

'I have other important matters to attend to in Paris,' said he whom they addressed as the Herr Rittmeister, 'and I shall return to Berlin on the afternoon plane. Be assured, gentlemen, that your good work will be reported to—you know who. Meanwhile—' again the ghastly smile—'perhaps you will wish to join me for a small drink of celebration, yes?'

They nodded eager assent.

'And where more suitable,' said the autocrat, 'than the Café des Deux Magots, which, by a pardonable stretch of fancy, might be described as the scene of your late triumph?'

On that unseasonably sunny morning, the snow was well on the way to slush, filling the gutters with grey torrents that marred the wings of the silver Rolls as Levy drew it to a halt outside the café.

The place, at that hour, was half empty of the art and intellectual élite of the capital—for such folk are not early risers as a genral rule. Henry Miller was at his usual table and scribbling away with the air of a man who has been at it all night long, occasionally taking a swallow of cognac, glancing sidelong with intense suspicion at anyone— Fosdyke and Levy included—who entered the café, and covering over his writing whenever anyone came within peeking distance.

The two conspirators took a table as far away from the rest of the clientèle as possible.

'Any news of the two—um—gentlemen we gave a lift to last night, Hal?' asked Fosdyke, after a swift glance over his shoulder.

'Not that I've seen. There was nothing in the morning papers.'

'That's right. I went out and bought them all first thing after I woke up.'

'Unless they were found almost immediately, they'd be too late to make the first editions.'

'I hadn't thought of that.'

Further speculation was cut short by the arrival of the waiter. They ordered coffee and croissants and Scotch on the side.

'Your good health, Hal,' said Fosdyke, raising his glass, but not too conspicuously. 'Here's to Art.'

'And to crime. I'll drink to both.'

'You were going to tell me about Nathan T. Willis's great

plan,' said Fosdyke, 'so that I should have a benchmark against which to pit my wits in devising another such. And I may say that my curiosity knows no bounds.' (He really was feeling quite muzzy, he told himself. But that could be attributed to the two Scotches he had already imbibed that morning from the sizeable hip flask that he had taken to carrying with him always ever since the great Authors' College débâcle.)

Hal Levy drained his glass and took a bite out of a croissant, the suave textural delight of which he had augmented with a heavy plastering of Normandy butter and apricot jam. Having washed it down with a swallow of café-au-lait, he said: 'I don't want you to be unduly inhibited by this account, Bernie. Nat Willis, like I've explained you, was a guy in a million, but in no ways superior in intellect and subtlety to your goodself—at least, that is my summation of your respective characters. And poor Nat's tragedy lay in that fact that he did not live to enjoy the fruits of our first big coup—nor, of course, any that followed, or will follow.'

Fosdyke let a solemn moment pass in silence, then he asked: 'What happened to him, Hal?'

'He fell overboard from the *Ile de France* in an Atlantic gale, while coming back from New York after smuggling the *Mona Lisa* into the States and collecting the fifty thousand bucks from our client.'

'Great Scott!' exclaimed Fosdyke. 'I hope he wasn't carrying the money about his person at the time?'

'Happily, no,' responded Levy. 'My share of the take was safely ensconced in the ship's safe in my name. Nat never trusted safes, but carried his share in a money belt, I guess, and it went down with him.' He called to the waiter to refill their glasses. 'Enough of repining for things that can't be undone,' he said. 'This is the story of how we stole the *Mona Lisa* . . .'

THE SWITCH

An Interlude

The day that Harold Hiram Levy met Nathan T. Willis after the latter had just executed a simple but effective confidence trick on an aged and gullible fellow American with baseball leanings, the artist took the trickster into his own confidence, showed him his copy of the *Mona Lisa*, told him frankly about the millionaire's proposition—and invited Willis to devise a means of making the switch and assisting in the operation on a fifty-fifty share-out basis. Willis—small, dark, mercurial, with a brash and engaging grin—accepted unhesitatingly; spent the whole of the following night sitting up in Levy's studio with a sheaf of rough writing-paper and six sharpened pencils, a coffee-pot and a carton of cigarettes. He had the answer by dawn.

That morning, Levy was able to wire his client that he was prepared to go through with the deal. By return came the following: AGREED STOP OSWALD ZEC SAILING LE HAVRE THURSDAY STOP HE WILL MONITOR DEAL STOP—CROESUS

This gave the two accomplices around a week to ten days to flesh out the bare bones of the plan. Working in shifts and employing a variety of simple disguises and changes of attire, they haunted the galleries of the Louvre museum during the periods of opening, and determined that Tuesday lunch-time between the hours of one and two appeared to be the slackest time of the week, when, not withstanding the manifest delights of tourist Paris, including the Louvre and the most famous picture in the world, almost everybody preferred—for some arcane reason which did not apply on any other day of the week—to enjoy their déjeuner. It was a conclusion that they were able to check again the following Tuesday, after Oswald Zec had arrived and all was set for the switch.

Zec, as has been implied earlier, was a man whose whole life was predicated on the premise that the entire set-up of the world, as devised by the Almighty, was a colossal conspiracy to bring about the downfall of Oswald Zec. For suitable remuneration, he was also prepared to accept that certain others might be included as victims of this galactic machination, and stood convinced that Levy's and Willis's true intent was to swindle his employer Croesus (a code name that Levy and the man in question had devised earlier). It was a not unreasonable assumption.

Thus, then, with the timing of the switch fixed, and the monitor arrived, they swung into action on the Tuesday after . . .

At a quarter to one, Willis and Zec, with Willis driving, arrived by the Louvre in a shabby 1926 Renault saloon that they had bought cheaply for cash from a kerbside trader in the Porte des Lilas. The actual parking spot, which had been carefully worked out within ten yards or so, was vacant. (If it had not been, they would have aborted the operation till the following Tuesday, so critical was the positioning.) Having parked, Willis, who was wearing a capacious mackintosh, got out and entered the museum, paying his five francs admission and wandering up into the galleries with a catalogue in his hand, just like any tourist. He left behind him the still highly suspicious Zec, and, propped up against the back seat, the spurious Mona Lisa draped in a cloth of a curious sort. Allowing ten minutes to go past, Zec then walked away from the Renault, having first lifted the car's bonnet and made a certain small adjustment to an ancillary part of the engine that made it incapable of being started.

Precisely at one, Levy arrived on the scene in another nondescript car that they had bought (he did not yet own one of his own; the Rolls of which he was so inordinately proud was paid for out of the proceeds of the *Mona Lisa* operation), and parked it about fifty yards further from the entrance to the museum than the Renault. He got out of the car and, without locking it, walked down and went into the museum, totally ignoring Zec, who was lurking at the foot of the steps by the entrance with the air of a man waiting for someone who was rather irritatingly late for a rendezvous.

The moment for the switch was fast approaching . . .

Levy made a swift tour of the galleries, noting that the paucity of visitors conformed to the usual Tuesday lunch-time pattern. On the way through, he walked past his accomplice without exchanging so much as a glance, though he answered the latter's cough with a clearing of his throat —prearranged signals for the immediate commencement of the operation.

As both men had appreciated in their walk-through, the long gallery in which their quarry was hung was now entirely empty of visitors—though it was not likely to remain so for ever. Empty—save for a uniformed attendant who stood by the archway leading into the gallery. There was another such guardian stationed at the very far end, but, as they had already established, this functionary had a foot patrol between there and the limit of the gallery beyond.

They took up position: Willis standing in front of the *Mona Lisa* and reading her up in his catalogue; Levy promenading slowly along the opposite side, looking up at the pictures, and moving towards the attendant. A glance over his shoulder to see the other attendant move off on his foot patrol—and he gave a cough.

This was the signal for—*action!*

Five paces and two pictures from the attendant, Levy gave an exclamation and, raising a hand to his right eye, made much play about it having become the recipient of a foreign body. He then produced a handkerchief and dabbed at the offending object, muttering all the time.

The attendant—an old soldier copiously hung about with campaign medals—made sympathetic noises and offered the suggestion that the trouble might lie with an inturned eyelash. Levy agreed that this might be so, and made

some shift to deal with it. Inevitably, the old poilu stepped
forward, put on his reading glasses and essayed to help. It
was almost the last thing he knew for ten minutes or so: a
chloroform pad pressed against his nose and mouth removed
him from all doubts and fears.

Next, having dragged the unfortunate out of sight of his
comrade whenever the latter reappeared at the far end of
the gallery, the conspirators took down the *Mona Lisa,* which
is executed in oil.paint upon a wooden board 30-plus inches
by nearly 21 inches—about the size of a large serving tray.

That done, Willis stripped off the voluminous mackintosh,
revealing that he was wearing underneath the full habili-
ments of a Parisian waiter of the classic sort: with swallow-
tail coat, starched collar and shirt front, black bow tie,
patent leather shoes, white ankle-length apron. Then, from
the pockets and environs of the capacious mackintosh they
produced several interesting items, including a traycloth
with elaborate lace edging.

The attendant who collected the admission tickets at a
barrier some twenty paces or so from the main entrance did
not give the blonde giant in the voluminous mackintosh a
second glance when the latter brushed past him, walked
slowly down the corridor and turned left to go out into the
sunshine.

The personage who followed shortly after commanded his
whole attention.

It was—unaccountably—a waiter bearing a tray, upon
whose dazzling white napery were set a bottle of champagne
and two tall glasses, a silver salver covered with a lid,
various items of cutlery and two plates. And one perfect red
rose poised to distraction in a specimen glass.

The functionary stared in blank astonishment at a vision
that he had never before seen in the precincts of the Louvre
museum, and a question teetered on his mystified lips.

It was answered before delivered.

The waiter paused by him and winked. 'Déjeuner pour Monsieur le Directeur,' he said confidingly.

'Ah, oui?' responded the other, puzzled the more.

'Et pour son amie,' added the other, and winked again.

'Ah, vive l'amour,' was the attendant's automatic response.

It is a fact that the human mind takes hold of first impressions and holds on to them for some time as unalterable truths—provided that they have been convincingly implanted. Few people will challenge what on the face of it they *assume* to be established fact. So it was with the ticket-collector. He saw, he heard, and for a short while he accepted the situation as presented to him. Some seconds passed before the inherent fallacies unloaded themselves in his mind; things like: the 'waiter' should not have come from the direction he did because there are no kitchens in the upper floors of the Louvre; the gallery director being a notorious woman-hater could not possibly be taking luncheon with a girlfriend—and, anyhow, his office did not lie in that direction.

But by the time those few seconds had passed, the conspirators had virtually won game, set and match!

'Eh, vous—monsieur—'alt!'

Too late, he shouted the challenge. Willis, by now abreast of the main door, made a sudden dart to the left and disappeared from sight, tray, contents and all.

The ticket-collector set off in hot pursuit.

Through the door and down the steps ran the outraged functionary. Half way down, he ran full into a man coming up. The latter, hopelessly entangled in the task of folding up a large and recalcitrant street map, appeared not to see the pursuer till they met in headlong collision. There was much offering and accepting of apologies, a disentanglement, and both went on their ways. Zec—for the juggler with the street map was he—paused at the top of the steps to see the chagrin in the ticket-collector's face as he stood and watched the 'waiter' jump into a car parked some distance away, saw the vehicle leap to life and tear off into the distance at top speed.

The alarm was raised. It was not till they found the 'undoubted' *Mona Lisa* lying in the back of the 1926 Renault parked only a few yards from the entrance, and took in the significance of the lace-edged traycloth draped over it, and the jumble of cutlery, plates, glasses, champagne bottle, not to mention the one perfect red rose, that they realized that the Louvre had been within an ace of being robbed of its prime possession.

Clearly, the miscreant, having dumped his 'tray' in the back, had tried to start the Renault and make his getaway, but to no avail. Upon examination, the car was found to have developed a minor electrical fault that precluded ignition. Fortunately for himself, the thief had taken the precaution of having an accomplice waiting with a second car in case of such an eventuality. Or so the museum people declared, nodding sagely in their wisdom.

The *Mona Lisa* was replaced on the wall, and everyone breathed a sigh of relief.

Notwithstanding the electrical fault, which had been the prime agent of thwarting the attempt, it was conceded that the prompt action of the ticket-collector, one Fouché, had greatly inconvenienced the thief and made him panic. In token of this service, the Society of Arts & Sciences presented Fouché with their Medal of Commendation, Third Class— an honour which so went to his head that he was emboldened to leave his nagging wife and elope to the Midi with a barmaid twenty years his junior.

Next day, Willis and Zec smuggled the real *Mona Lisa* out of France in a packing case marked *Glass—Fragile*.

The rest is—to coin a phrase—unrecorded history.

CHAPTER 6

By the time Harold Hiram Levy had finished his account of the *Mona Lisa* coup, the café had fairly filled up. Gertrude Stein was at her usual table and was holding forth to her acolytes in repetitive dactyls. Henry Miller was still scribbling away.

'It's marvellous—astounding,' said Fosdyke. 'And, at bottom, quite ridiculously simple. One wishes one had thought of it. Hal, quite frankly, I can't see myself coming up with a little gem of an idea like that. And you say that the authenticity of your copy—*which still hangs in the Louvre*—has never been questioned in the four years it's been there?'

'To my knowledge, never once,' replied Levy. 'Indeed, a couple of years ago it was earmarked to be included in a representative exhibition of Florentine art of the quattrocento in its native city—only they couldn't find an insurance company who'd cover it—not for any money in the world.'

'Astonishing,' said Fosdyke, 'truly astonishing. Mind you, Hal, as regards the switch, there must have been one or two sticky moments. What if, for instance, the ticket-collector had challenged—*really* challenged—Nathan Willis at the barrier? What then?'

'Nat had his psychology right,' replied the other. 'He said it was never in doubt but that the guy's delayed reaction would give him time to get out of the building, and so it was.

'Timing was the key. And the critical piece of timing was fixing it so that the ticket-collector saw Nat dive into my car *minus* the *Mona Lisa*—which I'd already taken from him and thrown in the back. That was the lynchpin of the whole operation: *no one saw but the one picture!*'

Fosdyke was about to add another comment when a newsboy came into the café shouting 'Extra'.

'That could be news of our two friends,' muttered Levy.

Fosdyke bought two copies of the paper and passed one to his companion. They were not long in finding what they sought: a five-line piece in the Stop Press.

'Oh my God!' breathed Fosdyke, when he saw the headline.

The headline ran: POLICE OFFICERS MURDERED.

' "In the early hours of this morning," ' read Levy, ' "a patrolling police officer discovered the bodies of two men on a bench in the Champs Elysées. Both had been shot in the back . . ." '

' "Their names are given as Inspector Alphonse Gaspardo and Officer Hyacinthe Delon, both of the Paris Police Department." '

The two conspirators met each other's gaze.

'This calls for another drink,' said Levy. 'And make mine a double.'

'We're up to the neck in it now,' said Fosdyke at length.

'You've never been so right in your life,' said the other. 'To catch a cop-killer, the flat-footed gentry of this world will go that extra mile, leave no stone unturned, put a shoulder to any wheel that offers itself, and lay a hand to any plough. Brother, that madame had it right when she said those two guys had powerful friends who'd stop at nothing for vengeance. And we have neatly put ourselves at the receiving end.'

'We could go to the police and make a clean breast of the whole thing,' suggested Fosdyke.

'We could,' conceded Levy. 'That might save us both from the guillotine—just. But how do you feel about spending the rest of your life vacationing in the tropical paradise of Devil's Island as an accessory after the fact?'

Fosdyke shuddered. 'Hal, what shall we *do*?' he whispered.

'We keep our heads down,' replied the other. 'I think

maybe the Rolls is a mite too conspicuous, so I'll garage her till our business is finished in Paris. Nothing—nothing at all—must interfere with our operation. Agreed?'

'Oh yes—*yes!*' affirmed Fosdyke, who had by then accustomed himself to the notion of being the possessor of half a million dollars and had no intention of trying to sell encyclopædias again.

Levy glanced at his watch. 'Right now,' he said, 'I'm going back to the studio to work on the picture, which is near to completion. You have your lunch date with your little amie, and I urge you to forget our slight predicament and enjoy yourself. When you're through, come around to the studio.' He scribbled a couple of lines on a paper napkin. 'Here's the address. No hurry. Take your time if you're having fun. You'll find me hard at work when you arrive.

'Let's go.' He left his carnation buttonhole—which was getting rather tired-looking—in the ashtray.

In a shop doorway across the boulevard from the café, three dark-clad figures watched and waited—as they had watched and waited since espying the distinctive silver Rolls-Royce Silver Ghost parked close by the entrance to the Deux Magots—one of them in mounting fury that bid fair to explode, his companions in sinking despair.

The ever-moving traffic constantly obliterated the door of the café from their view. The next time the line of vision was clear, two men had emerged and were standing at the kerb close by the Rolls. They were deep in conversation. Presently they shook hands and the tall blond got into the silver automobile.

'Himmel! I do not believe it!' breathed he of the moustache and rimless glasses.

'Herr Rittmeister, on my mother's head, I swear we saw them both fall!' wailed his companion.

'Blockheads! Pig-dogs!' blazed the autocrat. 'You shot the wrong men last night!'

With the frenzy of desperation, both functionaries groped in their armpits.

'Not here, you dolts!' cried the other, his voice rising to a muted scream. 'Not here in broad daylight with all Paris looking on! Get after them! Don't lose them! Keep me informed at the Hotel Crillon by telephone!'

His lackeys departed to do his bidding: he of the moustache and glasses to hail a cab and follow the Rolls, while his comrade to set off on foot in the wake of Bernard Fosdyke.

He whom they called the Herr Rittmeister remained in the shop doorway, his scarred face working.

When Sanson arrived at the Quai des Orfèvres that morning, he was greeted by Officer Guitry. Guitry, a Breton from Brest, had become Sanson's secretary and dogsbody when he transferred out of the uniformed branch, lured by the exciting lives that detectives no doubt lead. By now the young officer was well on the way to disillusionment.

'Chief, Madame Sanson rang, and will you phone her immediately? It's urgent.'

'Later, later,' responded Sanson. 'Anything new on the killings?'

'Not much, Chief. The officer who reported the finding says that there were tyre tracks in the snow, on the footpath close by the bench where he discovered the bodies, but they had thawed out before we had time to get a photographer and lights fixed up.'

'Were Gaspardo and Delon on duty last night while they were out?'

'No, Chief. More likely . . .'

'Well? Come on . . . out with it, lad!'

'Ah—the story's going the rounds of the building that they were out "putting on the screws".'

Sanson nodded. He knew only too well—had guessed all along—that the partnership of Gaspardo and Delon had been up to more than police work. Honest detectives do not walk around in handmade suits, nor drive smart cars and flaunt expensive-looking girlfriends in the night clubs of the faubourg. He sighed.

'Guitry, take a note,' he said. 'To all officers—search and question in every bar, nightclub, brothel, second-hand car dealer's, liquor store, and every freelance pimp and prostitute in the area covered by the dead officers. I want to know who was being squeezed. It should be apparent from a certain lightness of heart around the area this morning, an air of having shaken off an intolerable burden on the communal purse, and maybe someone will squeal, if only to preserve his neck from the lunette at the expense of somebody else's. Did Gaspardo and Delon have any money —big money—on them when they were found?'

'No, Chief. Only a couple of hundred francs in their wallets.'

'Then there was no pay-off last night,' mused Sanson. 'Or, at least, the victim, or victims, paid off in lead!'

Guitry went off to pass the commissaire's orders along the line, and Sanson slumped down in his chair, eyeing the telephone that stood before him on the desk. Upright, immobile, strangely menacing with the bell-like mouthpiece at the end of its tall neck, it put him in mind of a cobra reared up and about to strike. By easy stages, hesitatingly, he picked it up and asked the exchange to give him his own home number.

' 'Allo?'

'What do you want me for, Mathilde? I'm very busy.'

'You dirty dog! You filthy swine! I should have listened to my dear father. He told me to have nothing to do with you, and he was right!'

Sanson remembered with some wry amusement how his father-in-law, a pillar of the parish church and member of the village council, had taken him, Sanson, to his favourite brothel in the nearby town and introduced him to all the girls.

'Well, what is it now, Mathilde?' he asked.

'Who is Ginette Demauney, 10 bis, Rue Barbette?' she demanded, after the manner of Genghis Khan interrogating a prisoner on the bed of nails.

In twenty years of marriage to Mme Sanson and half as long again in the Department hobnobbing with the criminal fraternity, the commissaire had learned the best response to such a question, and that response was: deny everything.

'Never heard of her.'

'Then what is her name and address doing on a piece of paper hidden at the bottom of your collar-box? Tell me that!'

Not so easy. Think carefully before you answer, M. le Commissaire.

The Rue Royal, when he got there, held all the promise of spring: the midinettes danced about their errands, winning approving looks from pouchy-eyed flâneurs; the busy taxi-cabs honked their way in and out of the lines of traffic, earning cheerful curses from their fellow knights of the road; a horse-drawn delivery van, bright as a carousel, jogged past, wheels humming, high stepping. It needed only for the chestnut trees to be in blossom. Fosdyke's heart sang.

He entered the café and took his seat at the table where they had sat before. She was not there; he had not expected her to be, for he was a quarter of an hour early.

'M'sieur désire?' It was the waiter Jean, he who had chased him as far as the Concorde. He did not appear to bear any ill-will, though there was clear recognition in his eyes.

Fosdyke ordered Scotch on the rocks and addressed himself to waiting with all the patience he could muster, which, given the circumstances, was not a tremendous amount.

At one minute to zero hour, he had entirely convinced himself that she was not coming. As the minute hand of his watch swept inexorably towards the fatal spot—and he was staring down at it with a dull dread—a shadow fell across him. He looked up—and she was there.

'Hello.'

'Oh—hello. How nice to see you.' He leapt to his feet and overturned the chair next to him. This caused a certain amount of confusion at the adjacent table, where a lady of uncertain years was drinking a Pernod. Her pet poodle sat opposite. The poodle, being the occupant of the overturned chair, gave vent to its small fury in no mean manner, contingent upon which Fosdyke received a sharp nip in the ankle and was accused by the creature's fond owner of being an assassin and a communist. But all was presently settled.

Flushed, confused, Fosdyke took his place before Dorothy Batthyány, and relished what he saw.

'How's your survey progressing?' she asked.

'It's finished,' he replied.

She was wearing a light coat of mid-blue over a print frock, with a silk scarf flung carelessly about her neck. Her crisp sable hair was imprisoned in a white beret.

'So soon? What are you doing now?'

'Waiting to hear if the publishers have accepted my novel,' he replied, and with some truth.

'Oh, so you're also a writer. How thrilling. Do tell.'

He ad-libbed the plot of the novel about Murdoch and the confidence trick with the petrol, just as he had told it to Hal Levy, just as he had ad-libbed it a score of times to anyone who cared to listen. He could have recited it in his sleep; reciting it, he was able at the same time to regard her and to give his speculations free rein.

She had turned up for the luncheon date. What did that signify—if anything? Not for the first time, he cursed the inherent shyness that had brought him, a man of middle years, to the summit of total ignorance in matters concerning the opposite sex.

Had he—in the current jargon—'clicked' with her? Or was she just curious about him? Or at a loose end, therefore glad of something to do, someone to talk to, to flesh out the hour of luncheon? Or was she, perhaps, merely hungry?

And then—there was the other thing . . .

'So,' he said, rounding off the outline of his novel, 'Murdoch's dream came true. The biggest part of his lifetime dedicated to one end—and he won for himself a paradise island in the South Seas.'

'Wonderful,' she responded. 'Absolutely great. Honestly, I can't see how they can possibly not publish it. I expect I shall have to pay to talk to you in a year's time when you're rich and famous.'

(In a year's time—did she think so far ahead into their acquaintance?)

'How about a spot of lunch?' he suggested.

'I'm starving.'

The restaurant part of the establishment was situated at the rear: a single row of banquettes set along a narrow gallery. They took their places at an empty table for four, facing each other. She flashed him an encouraging smile, but said nothing. Fosdyke took shelter behind a menu.

'What do you fancy?' he asked.

'You choose,' she replied.

The waiter—Jean—came up very coyly and placed a nosegay of early spring flowers, snowdrops and aconites, between them. He fussed for a moment, gazing from one to another, and departed humming.

'He thinks we're lovers,' said Dorothy Batthyány, causing Fosdyke to start with surprise and overturn a glass, which fortunately was empty.

'Well, I suggest we start with vegetable soup, since it's still quite chilly out,' he said hastily, to fill the awful void of silence which had fallen upon her—to his mind—astonishing observation. 'Followed by a minute steak, the trimmings, and then cheese. How about that?'

'Suits me fine.' She folded her hands and rested her chin

upon them, gazing at him from under her quite unbelievably long eyelashes.

'And what are you doing with yourself?' he asked. 'You told me you're a student of human nature. Do you do it as a full-time job?'

'Oh no. Strictly part-time.'

'Is it—hard work?'

(This was him steering the conversation towards the sticking point that would resolve his doubts about her, one way or the other, once and for all.)

'Hard work? Mmmm—yes, you could say that,' she replied, seemingly amused by the concept.

'What kind of work?'

She shrugged. 'Oh, the easy kind. I'm incorrigibly lazy. Left to my own devices, I never get up before midday.'

'I see,' he said.

She looked at him, her head on one side, interrogatively.

'Why did you say it like that?' she asked.

'Like—what?'

'Well, in a kind of "Ho-ho, so that's the kind of person she is"—type of voice.'

Thrown back on the defensive, Fosdyke could only mumble that this had not been his intent. Fortunately, the reappearance of Jean the waiter to collect their order smoothed over the awkward patch. They did not speak again till the soup was brought.

'Whereabouts in Paris do you live?' he asked, trying another tack in his inquiries.

'Oh, not far from here,' she replied.

'On your own?'

'Oh dear no.' She laughed. 'Believe it or not, I share with six other people.'

'Sounds rather overcrowded.'

'It is. We live in absolute squalor.'

(His mind flew to La Ronde. Was that it, then? Did she actually live and work in a maison de rendezvous? And was it just a side-line, allowing herself to be picked up by some chap in a cruising limousine? Was that her part-time job as a 'student of human nature'?

'Were you in time for your—ah—luncheon appointment yesterday?' he asked. 'I didn't delay you too long with my idle chatter?'

Her spoon paused half way on its journey to her lips. She looked at him evenly, and with a slight puzzlement. 'Yes, I was in good time, thanks,' she replied.

'Went somewhere glamorous and expensive, I suppose?'

'Yes, as a matter of fact we did.'

'Nice for you.'

'Very nice,' she said, and addressed herself to her soup.

He had a compulsion to probe further, and had the fancy that a new attack from an entirely different quarter might yield further confirmation of her life-style.

'I've an idea,' he said brightly. 'If you're free, why don't we take a cab to the Rodin museum and pay homage to your little girl in the straw hat?'

She looked up, her eyes suddenly dancing with pleasure, and Fosdyke suffered a pang of remorse and self-loathing that he should have doubted for one moment the purity and sweetness of the lovely creature seated before him. 'Oh, I would love to, Bernard,' she said.

('Bernard'—she had addressed him by his name for the first time!'

'Well then,' he said, 'let's . . .'

She frowned, and the light went out of her eyes. 'Only I can't,' she said. 'Not this afternoon.'

'Oh, if you've got more important things on hand,' he said, 'forget it. It's of no consequence.'

'Oh, but it is of consequence, Bernard, and I truly would come with you, but I've an appointment that I simply can't break. It wouldn't be—kind—to break it, just like that.'

'What sort of appointment?' he demanded.

Her expression was indecipherable to Fosdyke, ignorant

as he was of the ways of women. 'I don't think you should ask me that,' she said quietly.

'Not unconnected with your part-time studies into human nature, I shouldn't wonder,' he grated.

'Something like that,' she said. And looked down into her empty soup plate.

They sat in complete silence, while several people came and went up and down the aisle. Glancing round, Fosdyke saw Jean the waiter arriving with their steaks, which he laid on a serving table nearby and busied himself in stirring the sauce to go with them.

Suddenly, she got up. 'Excuse me, please,' she said in a small voice. He stood up in unison and sat down again, turning to watch her small and shapely form pass down the aisle and out of his sight.

Jean came up, laid two plates at their places and brought the serving dish with the sizzling steaks.

'Madame 'as gone?' he asked.

'She'll be back in a minute,' said Fosdyke. 'You might as well serve.'

'Hokay.'

Dorothy had not returned by the time both plates were fully charged. Fosdyke sat and fidgeted for a few minutes, then signalled to Jean.

'I think it would be a good idea if you put these on the hot plate till Madame returns,' he said.

Jean shrugged. 'Hokay.'

A quarter of an hour later—and no Dorothy—Fosdyke called for his bill, which Jean wrote out with the air of a man copying an inscription from a tombstone.

'Madame, she is not coming back, hein?' he essayed.

'No, she's not coming back,' replied Fosdyke.

'Tant pis—too bad.' He took Fosdyke's banknote and gave him the change. He then removed the nosegay of early spring flowers from the table and sighed.

Fosdyke walked out of the restaurant and into the wintry

sunshine of the Rue Royale with a dull feeling of irremediable loss and the sense of having wilfully thrown away something infinitely precious.

He was entirely unaware of the individual in the black leather overcoat, pork-pie hat and mittens who had risen from his seat at a table three removes away and followed him out of the restaurant—and was now dogging his footsteps back towards the Left Bank.

Levy's studio, according to his directions, was on the top floor of a house in the Rue Guénégaud, which opens out at the Pont Neuf and is about ten minutes' walk from the Café des Deux Magots. Fosdyke trudged all the way there, sunk in his bitter gloom.

He found the house with some difficulty, for many of the buildings in that narrow, tall-walled street were not numbered. There was no sign of a concierge. A door leading off the central court brought him to the foot of a broad staircase that wound its circular way up through the core of the old building, and was suffering from a discernible sag at the outward end, so that one had the feeling, all the time, that the whole contraption was going to wrench its inboard end away from attachment to the walls and go plummeting down into the stairwell far below.

Two floors—three—four. Fosdyke's footfalls sounded hollow on the bare boards—and so did those of someone who was coming up behind him a couple of floors below.

He reached the top at last, and found himself breathing heavily from the effort. Only one door presented itself, and he knocked upon the woodwormed oak and waited.

No reply. He tried again. Same result. Levy, he fancied, must be out, and had probably left the place unlocked and a message inside. He turned the handle and the door creaked open to his touch.

There was a skylight immediately opposite him, and the bright afternoon sun blazed through it into his face, temporarily blinding him to the shadowed interior of the attic room.

And then he saw Levy.

His accomplice was seated in a chair against the wall under the skylight, staring across at him with an expression that mutely screamed to him to cut and run.

The reason for his silence was plain to see: standing beside his chair was an individual in a long black leather coat. He was holding the muzzle of a pistol close against the American's left ear.

'Good God—Hal!' cried Fosdyke, starting forward.

He strode only one pace—and then the swung butt of a pistol took him behind the ear and he pitched forward into a pit of darkness that receded away beneath his feet to an infinity of oblivion.

He was rising up from the sea-wrack, and there was a moaning in his ears that resolved itself into the murmuring of voices in a foreign tongue that he finally sorted out as being German. Next, his eyes sharpened into vision, and he was staring up into three blankly-regarding faces that looked down on him.

'Sprechen Sie Deutsch?'

'No—I don't have any German,' replied Fosdyke. He made an effort to raise himself up on one elbow, but a booted foot came out, was planted against his chest and thrust him back against the floor.

'Don't try to be cute, Bernie,' came Levy's voice from just outside his vision. 'These guys are playing for real.'

Levy was still seated in the chair. The two men in black leather were carrying pistols with silencers fitted. The third member of the trio—he of the monocle—spoke again:

'So, we have found you at last,' he said, addressing Levy, 'and how do I address you? Is it Professor Fortescue-Brown, or Lord Aberathney? Or are you today the excellent Mr H. Higgins, posing as a retail fruiterer, who sold my—*my principal*—a genuine Rembrandt, a Van Dyck and two Pieter de Hoochs for ten thousand marks?'

'Cheap at the price,' said Levy. 'A real snip. Taking seventeenth-century prices into account, that wouldn't have kept those fine artists in shoe leather.'

'Fakes—all!' snarled the German.

'You don't say? You surprise me.'

'Upon examination,' said the other, 'one of the Pieter de Hoochs was found to have been painted on unseasoned American pine.'

'It's a fair cop,' said Levy with a shrug. 'I got careless, knowing I was dealing with pig-ignorant Philistines.'

The monocle all but fell from the other's frozen eye, and the gold-filled fangs were bared in fury. He made a gesture to his henchmen to gun down the figure in the chair, but changed his mind. 'I think,' he said, 'that we will dispatch Mr H. Higgins rather more slowly when his time comes, which will be soon.' So saying, the man they called the Herr Rittmeister turned his back on his victim-to-be, skirted the prostrate Fosdyke, and strode round the attic room, peering up at the paintings which lined the walls and stood upon easels; fastidiously avoiding tables, stools and workbenches that were littered with the detritus of the painter's life: palettes plastered with spectra unmentionable, gobbets of dry paint splashed everywhere, filthy rags, bottles of oil and turpentine, mahl sticks, brushes, brushes, brushes everywhere. And, at the far end of the room, so positioned as to benefit from the south light that filtered suavely through a wide, grimy window, the tallest and widest easel of them all, over which was hung a concealing velvet cloth.

'And what have we here, hein?' he mused.

Reaching up, he wrenched aside the covering and threw it to one side.

'Himmel!' he exclaimed. 'Wunderbar!'

A new light had entered that dingy room—the light of unworldliness that shone from out of a sky of an illimitable blue, and seeped in through the nooks and crannies of gnarled and tumbled rocks, pointing up the foreground figures and bathing them in a golden glow. Two infants and a winged angel crouched there by the kneeling figure of the Madonna, whose calm, elegant hand was stretched as if in blessing upon her only child. And her robe was blue like the sea beyond the rocks.

A silence had fallen upon the five men in the attic room. Fosdyke, who had drawn breath in a gasp of awe and astonishment to see the vision of eternity suddenly revealed, exhaled silently, lest the sound seem like sacrilege.

The Herr Rittmeister slowly turned to look at the man in the chair. His pointing finger was directed at the painting.

'Is that—*your* work?' he asked.

'Done with my own fair hand,' replied Levy.

'It is—*fantastic!*'

'Blame Leonardo, not me. I just made the copy.'

The autocrat tapped his scarred cheek. 'When we have —dispatched you and your accomplice, my friend, I shall take this picture back to Germany for my—principal. It will go some way towards recompensing him for the fraud that you perpetrated.'

He gave a curt order to his henchmen, upon which they went forward with the obvious intention of taking the picture down from the easel.

'Don't touch it!' shrieked Levy. 'Some of the goddamned paint's still wet,' he added.

The Herr Rittmeister motioned to his men to desist. 'And when will it be dry?' he demanded.

'Oh, tomorrow—the next day,' said Levy. 'Mind you, I have to tell you that the picture isn't quite finished yet. It still has to be given the authentic touches of age and discolouration that will make it a faithful copy of the original in the Louvre.' He grinned hopefully. 'So you'll have to keep me alive for a while yet, to finish the job. Also my assistant—' indicating Fosdyke—'who's an expert at grinding and mixing pigments in the quattrocento manner.'

'That will not be necessary,' responded the other coldly. 'My principal will be quite satisfied with the painting as it stands, without the authentic touches of age and discolouration. I think we shall dispose of you both now and return for the painting tomorrow, or the next day.' He nodded to his henchmen and drew the palm of his hand edge-wise across his throat in a gesture that called for no elaboration of meaning.

Two silenced pistols were produced and cocked—snick-snick!

'In payment for *The Virgin of the Rocks,* I will grant you the benefit of a merciful end, ' declared the autocrat.

Two pistols were brought up to aim: one at Levy, the other at Fosdyke. The latter closed his eyes.

'*No! Stop! I've got a million dollar proposition!*' From Levy.

A brusque word from the Herr Rittmeister and the weapons were lowered—with some show of regret from both parties concerned.

'Is this a trick?' demanded the autocrat.

Levy shook his head. 'This is on the level,' he assured the other. 'Listen: how would your principal like to own the real and authentic *Virgin* from the Louvre museum, the which is so valuable that there isn't an insurance company in the whole wide world that would put a price on it for valuation?'

'You are joking, of course.'

Levy shook his head. 'Not so. I am in the process of painting this copy—with the assistance of my friend and colleague Dr Fosdyke here—with a view to making an exchange that will never be detected. We walk in with the copy. We walk out with the real thing. And no one will be any the wiser!'

'Absurd!' sneered the German. 'How could this be done? You would be detected as soon as you crossed the threshold.'

'It *can* be done, and it *will* be done!' declared Levy. 'A foolproof method has been devised by Dr Fosdyke. Isn't that right, Doc?'

Fosdyke opened his mouth to reply, but his throat was so dry from terror that nothing would come. He merely nodded vigorously and made a noise—anything, anything, to win for them both a lease of life, however tenuous.

'Tell me more,' demanded the autocrat.

CHAPTER 7

The barrier, the watershed, between hostile suspicion and a benign condition that only overwheening euphoria can engender was greatly assisted by the production of a bottle of fine malt whisky, with which Levy proceeded to ply the Herr Rittmeister—and he never stopped talking all the time —save to answer an occasional question.

'Then this plan—this scheme to replace the real picture with the false—it cannot fail?' questioned the autocrat.

'In basic terms, it is foolproof,' Levy assured him. 'There still remain some details to be justified one with the other. Dr Fosdyke, in addition to being the greatest living expert on quattrocentre pigments, is also a mathematician of international standing, as you will doubtless know . . .'

The Herr Rittmeister gravely inclined his head in assent, and took another swallow of the excellent malt.

'Tonight, and for the rest of the time that I am putting the authentic touches to the painting, he will be at work with his slide rule, his logarithms, astrolabes, azimuths, and other arcane adjuncts of his science. By the time we are ready to act, the great scheme will practically work itself.'

The German drained his glass. 'Good!' he said. 'I accept the proposition in principle. You, Herr Higgins, will complete the painting in all respects. The Herr Doktor . . .' and he bowed stiffly towards Fosdyke—'will complete his arrangements. We will leave you now, but my followers—' he indicated the glowering henchmen—'will keep you under surveillance, day and night, till the operation is completed. One false move, the merest hint of treachery, any attempt to evade your watchers, and you will be eliminated with as little compunction as they would show in cracking a pair of fleas. 'Understood?'

'Yes,' said Levy.

'Perfectly understood,' said Fosdyke.

'You will telephone me when you have effected the exchange,' ordered the autocrat. 'The Hotel Crillon—Room 230.'

They listened to the footsteps of the three Germans recede down the rickety staircase and fade away into silence. Then they met each other's gaze.

'What—what have you let us in for?' breathed Fosdyke. 'You know jolly well that I haven't *begun* to figure out how to work the switch with the *Virgin*.'

'No matter,' responded the other. 'You'll have time to work on it while I'm finishing off the painting.'

'But—but you told that fellow that, so far as the idea went, it was all fixed save for a bit of titivation,' protested Fosdyke. 'But I don't have a basic notion!'

The big American laid a hand on his companion's shoulder. 'I bought us a little time, Bernie,' he said. 'Who knows what might happen in between? The guy with the monocle might fall under a bus. You and I might get struck by lightning. Or you might come up with a hot idea for the switch.'

They took seats side by side on a broken-down sofa. The winter's sun was setting, and the shadows were gathering in the attic room, softening the contrasts of light and shade in the picture of the Madonna, infants and angel.

'You see the problem, Bernie,' said Levy, nodding towards the painting. 'If the *Mona Lisa* is of the dimensions of a serving tray, this babe's more the size of a table—78

inches by 48 inches. Same as the other version in the
National Gallery, London.'

'Oh, Leonardo painted two versions, did he?'

'Sure. And, apart from a few superficial additions and
subtractions, identical. As I was saying, on the score of size
alone, we couldn't consider using the waiter gag again. This
new switch, Bernie, has got to be something fresh, original,
utterly audacious, totally stunning!'

'It's a tall order, Hal,' said Fosdyke lugubriously.

'I'm in your corner and rooting for you, Bernie,' responded the other. 'By the way, how did you make out with
your little amie over lunch?'

'Don't speak of it,' said Fosdyke.

'Bad as that, huh?'

'Worse.'

'I'll say no more.'

Oh, the longing, thought Fosdyke. The wish that one
could have the opportunity all over again. He had pressed
her too hard, that erring magdalen, when he should have
shown compassion, tolerance, forgiveness. His probing
tongue had cut into her defences, his caustic sarcasm ('Your
studies into human nature') had wounded her to the quick.
And now he would never see her again, for in all Paris, that
café was the place that she could avoid at all costs. And
there was nowhere else to look for her—save all Paris.

It was nearly dark now. Hal Levy was slumped beside
him, brooding. Outside the window, the rooftops of the city
were growing pinpoints of light from a thousand garret
windows; windows behind which pictures were being
painted, words written, meals cooked and eaten, love and
passion made flesh. Across the river, in a shuttered house
in a narrow street, Madame and Yvonne, Marie, Solange
and the rest of the girls were settling down to another
night of champagne and commercial sin. Somewhere in a
municipal morgue, Inspector Gaspardo and Officer Delon
were sleeping the second night of their eternal rest, the look

of mild surprise still on their uncomely faces. Heaven knows what the insufferable swine with the monocle and the scar was up to.

And there, before him, *The Virgin of the Rocks,* in all her perfection . . .

It came to him, then: like the beginning of a great theme by Beethoven: slowly and tentatively at first, teasing a little, advancing and retreating; till it burst upon the mind and the emotions, unquestioning and unquestionable, starkly irresistible—like the thunder of great waves pounding on a barren shore.

'*I've got it!*' he shouted. "*I know how to work the switch!*'

He told his companion in half a dozen sentences. It was simplicity itself at bottom—but hung about with detailed complications that would have to be ironed out. Levy saw this clearly—but rejoiced.

'By thunder!' he cried. 'I knew you had it in you. I knew all along!'

Following the commissaire's orders, all the available detectives of the Quai des Orfèvres had been on the job since mid-morning. Not a commercial enterprise of the kinds that Sanson had particularized was missing in a concerted sweep through the area lately policed by the team of Gaspardo and Delon—and many an incidental can of worms was prised open during the operation. When Sanson returned to headquarters in the late evening, a dozen or so men and women were crowded disconsolately in the waiting-room under guard.

'Who are these?' Sanson asked of his secretary-dogsbody.

'They were picked up during the sweep, Chief,' replied Guitry, referring to the notes on his clipboard. 'During the search, we unearthed two cases of harbouring narcotics, three illicit stills; the rear of the chemist's shop in the Rue Gaston Lefèvre is, you'll be surprised to hear, a homosexual brothel; and the Ritz garage in the Impasse Périgord takes in hot cars and gives them new bodies. But that isn't the best bit . . .'

'What,' asked Sanson with commendable patience, thinking of all the extra work that the sweep had brought in, and he desperately short of manpower, 'what is the best bit?'

'The type who runs a bar at the corner of the Place d'Amsterdam had a wife and mother-in-law who were supposed to have run out on him and gone back to St Loup-sur-Semouse. Our fellows found their bodies floating in a couple of cognac casks in the cellar, fresh as daisies.'

All this while the pair of them were walking towards the commissaire's office, the door of which Guitry opened for his chief to enter. 'Anything on the killers of Gaspardo and Delon? I would point out that this was the object of the operation.'

'Nothing much, Chief, and mostly of the negative sort. But Sergeant Duval has a theory.'

'Send for Duval.'

Sergeant Duval and Sanson had joined the police at the same time, and the Wheel of Chance that dictates the lives and careers of men with superficially similar abilities had greatly differenced their advancements in the years between. It said much for the characters of the two former rivals for promotion that only Sanson felt any embarrassment when they were together.

'Well, Duval, what's the theory?' asked the other.

'I reckon they're all in it together,' replied Duval. 'Or most of them. The brothel-keepers, café owners, the rest. It's my view that Gaspardo and Delon were putting on the squeeze in a big way, so that their victims got desperate and formed a syndicate to pay for a killer—or killers.'

'Someone from outside Paris, you think?'

'I would have thought so, chief—only, Nikki Lamartine has gone missing.'

'Has he now?'

Nikki Lamartine, a long-standing thorn in the side of the

Quai des Orfèvres, was a middle-weight gang boss who, with one eye on similar operations in far-off Chicago, dealt in extortion, prostitution, gambling and narcotics. And almost certainly murder.

'I remember the time,' said Duval, with a touch of nostalgia, 'when Nikki put the squeeze on Judge Bisset to get the case dismissed against the Lamartine gang's top hit-man.'

'That's right,' supplied Sanson. 'One of Nikki's girls was put on to Bisset, with the view to getting some compromising photographs.'

'Only Bisset's wife ran off to Menton with the girl,' said Duval. 'And Bisset had the greatest pleasure in sending Nikki's boy to the guillotine. I laughed for a week.'

'So Nikki's missing,' said Sanson. 'That could be a pointer to the way an innocent person would lie low till we find the killer—thus avoiding a rather rough interrogation as a suspect cop-slayer.'

Duval looked disappointed. 'So we do nothing?'

'By no means,' said Sanson. 'Put out a general call to the metropolitan area and the provinces. We'll have Nikki in and put on the squeeze. No rough stuff, mind. It doesn't look well in court.'

'Right, Chief.' Duval brightened. On the way to the door, he paused. 'Did I sell you a ticket for the Police Ball on Saturday?'

'We won't be going,' replied the other. 'The wife's—not very keen.'

'All right,' said Duval. In common with the rest of the commissaire's staff, he knew how things were with Sanson and his spouse.

Alone, Sanson addressed himself to the notes that Guitry had made on last night's arrests. He was still juggling with the forbidding scale of the problem when the phone rang.

''Allo? Oh, it's you, Mathilde.'

'I've caught you out now, you dirty dog! The last time you took that collar-box away was in November, when you attended the Interpol seminar in Deauville. I checked up, and there's a Rue Barbette in Deauville. 'So *that's* where you picked up your Ginette Demauney, you . . .'

Night-time over Paris.

In his suite in the Hotel Crillon, the autocrat prepared himself for bed. It was quite a ritual. Stripping to one-piece woollen combinations, he had then to unlace and remove the torturously cinched corset which maintained a semblance of the figure he had enjoyed in his younger days. Next, still retaining the combinations, he put on a short, frogged smoking jacket and inspected himself in a long mirror. Surprisingly, this garment was embellished with—in descending order—the white-black-white ribbon of the Iron Cross 2nd Class in the top but one buttonhole, the Iron Cross 1st Class on the left breast, with the pilots' badge of the old Imperial German Flying Corps underneath and slightly to one side. He then took from a leather case the highly prized order Pour le Mérite, which he hung around his neck on its black and silver-grey ribbon.

This done, he proceeded to the next part of the bedtime ritual, which entailed the opening of a leather photograph frame in the form of a triptych. The outer panels revealed scenes of a group of Fokker DVII aeroplanes of the Great War, both on the ground and in the air. The centre panel was of the autocrat himself, dressed in the uniform of captain (or, more correctly, Rittmeister, since, like the great von Richthofen, he had transferred from the cavalry to the air arm).

The autocrat next poured himself a generous measure of schnapps in a toothglass and pledged the memories embodied in the triptych with glass raised, following this by downing the fiery spirit in one swallow.

He climbed into bed just as he was, combinations, decorated smoking jacket and all. Propped up with pillows, he then took up his favourite reading: a well-thumbed American muscle-man magazine.

Later, he fell asleep with the magazine still on his knee, and his monocle still screwed firmly in place.

Bernard Fosdyke slept badly on the sofa, and woke with a foul taste in his mouth and the sensation that someone was about to jump on him from behind. Levy was still asleep with all his clothes on on the single bed at a corner of the garret, snoring peacefully. The Madonna in the painting continued her eternal blessing.

Yawning, Fosdyke went over to the window and drew aside the blanket that played the role of a curtain; the sudden sunlight woke his companion.

'Do you have to do that? What the hell time is it?'

'Nearly ten. If we want to get part one of the operation completed today, we'd best get started.'

'All right, all right.' Levy threw his legs off the bed and stood up with a groan. 'God, we must have killed that bottle of malt last night.'

'We did,' said Fosdyke. 'I think we should eat something to settle our insides. What do you have?'

'Scrambled egg suit you?'

'Fine.'

While the big American cooked scrambled eggs and coffee on a gas ring, Fosdyke bent his effort to composing a short letter on an antique, stand-up-and-beg typewriter which Levy must have last used in a previous incarnation, so thick was the dust, so convoluted the cobwebs snarled in and out of its primitive interior. By the time the coffee was brewed, the missive was finished. He passed it to his companion.

Levy read it and nodded. 'Great, great. The right touch. Not too pushy, not too obsequious. They'll buy it.'

Over breakfast, Fosdyke said: 'I still wish we could get some endorsement from the art establishment. I wonder if the avant garde really has any mileage at the Louvre museum.'

His companion washed down a mouthful of egg and toast

with a swig of coffee and belched delicately. 'Bernie,' he said, 'I have no pull with the art establishment, so you can forget that. On the other hand, I may still have the vestigial affection and respect of Gertrude and her circle—if only I'm able to fan that dead flame back into life with my inimitable charm. As to the influence of the avant garde in Paris of nineteen thirty-three, you may be sure that the art establishment, the Louvre museum included, may hold the avant garde in public scorn, but deep down inside it leaves them quaking in their boots—for in it they see their apocalypse.'

'We shall see,' replied the other, half-convinced.

Shortly after eleven o'clock, the two conspirators set off on foot for the Deux Magots, remarking to each other upon the figure in the black leather coat that detached itself from a doorway opposite and came after them. This same spectre (it was he of the moustache and glasses) also followed them into the café, settled himself at a table nearby, and was witness to the scene that followed.

'Don't look right now,' murmured Levy, 'but the gang's all here. We'll give it five minutes, and then saunter over. I'll introduce you to Gertrude and we'll take it from there. Okay?'

Fosdyke nodded, felt the adrenalin drip generously into his blood supply, and found himself drumming out a rhythm on the table top with his fingernails. He reached hungrily for the large Scotch that Levy had ordered.

The hum of conversation from the nearby table came to them clearly, dominated, as ever, by the cropped-haired woman of the commanding timbre.

'Versatile is versatile is versatile,' declared she. 'Jean's versatility in no way detracts from the force of his creativity. The critical success of *Le Sang d'un Poète* last year only underscores his former chef d'œuvre, which was to follow a regiment of marines to the front in nineteen-fourteen—and he medically unfit.'

This sally won her a round of laughter, and the subject of her discourse—a sharp-featured man in his forties with a shock of wavy hair—gave a pinched smile. 'Ma chère Gertrude,' he responded, 'you are right, as always. Creativity, in the sense of the pursuit of truth and beauty, made me follow those delightful boys in nineteen-fourteen.'

Levy drained his glass and squeezed his companion's arm.

'That, I figure, is our cue, Bernie,' he whispered. 'Let's go!'

Gulping down his own drink, Fosdyke got to his feet and followed his accomplice over to the other table. The woman Gertrude regarded the approaching giant with a frown of slight puzzlement, which cleared in a faint smile carrying a hint of patronage.

'Well, my friends,' she said. 'Speaking of versatility, here we have the egregious Mr Harold H. Levy, who combines a disconcertingly cunning skill as an academic painter with that of art critic. Pablo!'

At her call, a smallish, thick-set man at the table behind her paused in the act of slowly stroking the cheek of a pretty blonde and directed a pair of large, berry-black eyes upon the speaker.

'Pablo, my friend Levy once described your paintings as "the fumbled ravings of a myopic cannibal".'

The other gave a shrug of his powerful shoulders and went back to his stroking.

'However,' she resumed, 'I once had high hopes of directing Levy's quite remarkable creative intelligence towards more cerebral pursuits. Not so, my dear Levy?'

'Quite correct,' confirmed Levy. 'Ah—may I introduce my friend and colleague Dr Bernard Fosdyke, a Fellow of All Souls, University of Oxford. Winner of the Newdigate Prize and—as poet and art historian—a rising star in the firmament of the avant garde of British art.'

Fosdyke found himself and his spurious credentials being

A VIRGIN ON THE ROCKS

well-received by Gertrude and her table companions, who also included the burly American in the broad-brimmed fedora whom he had observed on his first visit to the café. Nevertheless, they were not invited to sit down, the autocratic leader of the circle obviously having determined that their status was that of standing acquaintances, notwithstanding which, she was discernibly more condescending towards Fosdyke's companion.

'You are keeping better company, my friend,' she declared. 'Can it be that your former exposure to my influence is having a belated effect?'

'It's likely,' conceded Levy. 'Leastways, I have joined Dr Fosdyke in an enterprise to bring together the two strains of the academic and the avant garde in a common dialogue.'

'Interesting,' replied the woman. 'The outcome of such a dialogue, if properly conducted, could only result in the collapse of the academic establishment into the arms of the avant garde.'

'That, Gertrude, is what Fosdyke and I have in mind,' purred Levy, and looked as devious and machiavellian as he was able.

'I approve,' declared the other. 'And if there is anything that I and my circle can do to forward your enterprise, you have only to say the word.'

'Well, as a matter of fact, there is.' Fosdyke experienced another effluence of adrenalin, as his fellow-conspirator took from his breast pocket the letter that he had composed on the typewriter that morning. 'Fosdyke and I would be greatly obliged if you would endorse our enterprise with what amounts to a letter of introduction. You see, to the people in Paris who *really* matter, I am scarcely known, and Fosdyke not at all.'

She took the letter and read it through. Fosdyke held his breath.

He need have had no qualms. She looked up from the missive and smiled. 'It is well said by those of the Christian persuasion,' she said, 'that there is more joy over one sinner that repents than over ninety-nine of the just—or words to that effect. In appreciation of your salvation, my dear Fosdyke, I will endorse this note, and so will my circle.' Whereupon, she scrawled her signature at the foot of the typed sheet.

'You next, Alice!' To her female companion.

'And now you, Jean . . . and you, Ernest.'

Both men named had dashing signatures, executed with much braggadocio—as if they were signing cheques for six figures.

'And you, Henry! *He-e-nry!*'

Henry Miller gave a guilty start, looked up from his notebook, and covered it with his hand when Levy brought the letter over to his table.

'Sign it, Henry.'

Henry obeyed and went back to his frenzied scribbling.

'Now you, Pablo.'

The last addressee had by now graduated to stroking the blonde's shoulder, in the furtherance of which enterprise he had unfastened the top button of her blouse. He signed the letter without looking round at it.

'Well, there you have it, Levy,' said Gertrude, with the air of a pagan queen delivering the death warrant of a thousand captives. 'And I have the notion that you came here this morning with the one intent of enlisting my aid in this matter. Correct?'

'You seek me out and find me, Gertrude,' said Levy.

'To find is to find is to find,' said she.

They almost ran out of the Deux Magots, and only slowed their step when they came to another café which was well off the main thoroughfare and a fair distance away from the scene of their recent triumph.

'We were well advised to get the hell out of that scene,' said Levy, when they had sat down and ordered large Scotches.

'Next thing, and they'd have been quizzing us as to details. And I'm not entirely sure of the function of a Fellow of All Souls, and neither are you, I shouldn't wonder.'

'We could just as well have forged the signatures ourselves,' grumbled Fosdyke, whose nerves were still stretched taut by the experience. 'For a chap who can duplicate the works of Leonardo da Vinci, it would have been no great chore.'

'Bernie, Bernie,' responded the other, 'to do such would have offended my sense of artistic unity. Besides, you never know, but that letter might get checked up on, and then where would we have been?'

'Of course, you're right,' admitted Fosdyke. 'Well, let's have a look at the thing and see how it reads, signatures and all.'

Levy took out the letter and laid it on the table before them both.

Paris, February 2nd, 1933

To Whom it may concern:

This letter introduces Dr Bernard A. Fosdyke, M.A., D. Phil. (Oxon.), a Fellow of All Souls and Member of the Royal and Imperial Foundation for the Arts, together with his colleague Mr Harold H. Levy, artist-painter, whose works hang in the Tate Gallery, London; the Guggenheim Museum; the Straits Art Gallery, Singapore; and in private collections worldwide.

Dr Fosdyke and Mr Levy are in Paris in the furtherance of a most exciting artistic project which they would like to discuss with you, and we are more than happy to endorse their impeccable bona fides.
(Signed)

Gertrude Stein	Ernest Hemingway
Alice B. Toklas	Henry Miller
Jean Cocteau	Pablo Ruiz y Picasso

'It would certainly convince me,' said Fosdyke.

'And it will also convince you-know-who,' said Levy, replacing the letter in his pocket and picking up his glass. 'Now, as to the next step—I'm going back to the studio to work on the picture and you are going to the Louvre to make a few discreet and oblique inquiries. What about lunch? Shall we grab something in the boulevard, or buy a couple of steaks and take them back to my place to cook?'

'I—I'll make my own luncheon arrangements, thanks, Hal,' replied the other with a certain evasiveness that was not lost on his companion.

'Please yourself, old chap.' Levy nodded towards the window, and to where, at the opposite side of the street, two black-clad figures were in conversation and looking across at the café. 'Amos and Andy are still on the job, I see. Be particularly careful not to shake either one of them off accidentally—not at this stage.'

Fosdyke looked at his watch, drained his glass and got up to go. 'I'll see you later, Hal,' he said.

'Take it easy, Bernie,' said the other. 'By the way, are you okay for folding money?'

'Mmmm, I'm fine, thanks.'

'When you run short, just say the word. I'm funding this operation, remember.'

'Thanks, Hal.'

He was gone. Levy shook his head and smiled. 'I certainly hope you haven't blown the deal completely and she turns up again today,' he mused out loud.

Fosdyke took a cab to the Rue Royale, and the shadowing Moustache and Glasses followed after in another.

Telling the driver to set him down at the end of the street, Fosdyke then got out and walked slowly towards the café, half-dreading, half-savouring every step that might lead him to joy or to disappointment. It also wanted half a minute to the specific hour.

Dead on time, he entered the café and looked towards

their table, which was occupied by an elderly couple who
looked as if they were up from the provinces. Seeking about
him with sinking heart, Fosdyke saw no sign of her whom
he so earnestly sought.

Jean the waiter came out of the kitchen bearing a
laden tray. He saw Fosdyke, paused—and shook his
head sadly.

There was nothing for it but to wend his way to the
Louvre, to follow the next step of the plan. There was no
point in waiting around—he had lost her for good.

CHAPTER 8

Fosdyke got back to the studio just after four o'clock, leaving
Moustache and Glasses on watch in the street outside, to
find his accomplice engaged upon a curious painting
chore.

The *Virgin* still stood upon her easel, and even with the
untutored eye, Fosdyke was able to discern the distinctive
signs of ageing, manifested in a darkening of the very dark
passages of paint, an overall obfuscation of the sort caused
by the application, through the centuries, of successive
layers of mastic varnish. In short, it had the traditional
'Old Master' appearance that is frequently taken to be
confirmation of the genuine article.

But Levy was not at that time concerning himself with
the spurious Leonardo. Instead, he was engaged upon the
curious task of painting depressed ovoid shapes upon the
whitewashed wall of the studio. This he did with a pointed
brush of fine camel hair, which he dipped from time to time
in a paint mix secreted in the lid of a fair-sized gunmetal
cigar box of the sort that a confirmed cigar addict carries
around in the breast pocket and contains five smokes.

He looked round when Fosdyke came in. 'Hi, Bernie,' he

greeted him, 'I'd like for you to time me over the course. Ready?'

'Ready,' confirmed the other, looking down at the second-hand of his watch.

'Say when.'

'GO!'

At the order, Levy advanced his ready-charged brush towards the wall; a brief hesitation, in which he determined size, shape, position—and in one clean movement he executed a perfect flattened oval shape the size of, say, a side plate. He stood back and appraised his handiwork, head on one side, eyes narrowed. He then looked round and compared it with the twenty or so similar side plates with which he had embellished the wall.

'How was that, Bernie?' he asked.

'Five seconds and a bit.'

'I have to get it down to under four, I reckon.'

Fosdyke examined the job closely. 'It's quite perfect,' he said. 'I wouldn't have believed that that oval had been painted freehand—and without pause.'

'It's a knack that I share with most of the old masters,' said Levy modestly. At least one of them—I think it was Raphael—when asked by a particularly stupid pope to produce evidence of his competence as an artist simply took out a pencil and drew a perfect circle on the wall. He got the job.

'Well, now, how did you get on at the Louvre?'

'I struck up an acquaintance with an old chap who sells postcards in the outer lobby of the gallery,' said Fosdyke. 'He was not unamenable to the offer of a drink, and I took him to a café in the Place du Louvre, where he grumbled about his job, the working conditions, the foreman set over him, and gradually, as I led him along by the nose and plied him with fines, about his boss, the director of the museum.'

'And . . .?'

'His is a stop-gap appointment, Hal. The former director,

it seems, retired last year laden with various degrees of the Légion d'Honneur, the Palmes Académiques, and a seat in the French Academy. This temporary chap—name of de Courcey—has held appointments in several provincial galleries. A civil servant and an ardent careerist, his ambition—so my drinking friend informed me—is to keep his nose clean, please all the right people, fall out with nobody, and have the appointment confirmed as permanent. To which end, he is willing and anxious to crawl and crawl again beyond the call of duty.'

Levy grinned. 'In other words, friend de Courcey was destined to be alive and well in this year of nineteen hundred and thirty-three for the sole reason of advancing our enterprise. Right?'

'That's how it struck me, Hal,' said Fosdyke. 'He could have been an intransigent old curmudgeon well ensconced in a job for life and to hell with everyone. Instead, we've got some pushy little chap on the make whose waking nightmare is to put a foot wrong and get sent back to the provinces . . .'

'. . . And you bet your sweet life he's got a pushy little wife who says if he goes back there he goes alone . . .'

'. . . So he paints her a picture of their life as Monsieur and Madame the Director of the Louvre Museum, with retirement on a princely pension after many years of distinguished service . . .'

'. . . With the Légion d'Honneur, the Palmes Académiques . . .'

'And a seat in the French Academy—don't forget that, Hal.'

'Here's to friend de Courcey, his imminent confusion and future distinction,' said Levy, grinning.

He returned to his plate-drawing, alternating the same with another figure: a sloping line about eighteen inches long surmounted by a shorter stroke set horizontally to its upright. He was able to paint this in slightly more than three seconds. While he was so engaged, his companion addressed himself to drafting a letter; when he had done, he called for Levy's attention.

'Tell me what you think of this, old chap,' he said. 'I've addressed it to the Director. "Dear Sir—The accompanying letter of introduction is self-explanatory. My colleague Mr Levy and I would greatly like to meet you to discuss various aspects of our project which may well be of interest to the Louvre museum and of considerable cultural and prestigious benefit to all parties. Might we suggest that you honour us by being our guest for a working dinner at the Tour d'Argent? We could offer you Monday, Tuesday or Wednesday evenings of next week, and would wish to wait upon you at your office at around, say, six o'clock."

'Is six o'clock too early, do you think, Hal?'

'No, no,' Levy assured him. 'A guy like de Courcey will leap at the chance of impressing us before we take him out to dinner. There'll be champagne and nibbles of caviar on blinis, you bet. Together with cut flowers on his desk and Cuban corona-coronas in an engraved silver cigar box for which the staff of his former museum were with difficulty persuaded to subscribe for his leaving present.'

'You like the touch of the Tour d'Argent?'

'Sure! I love the grand gesture—particularly when it costs nothing. Though I suppose we'd better book a table—just in case.'

Fosdyke laughed. 'Right, I'll type this out and post it right away, so that it will be on his desk at the Louvre tomorrow morning. And you, Hal?'

'I'll carry on with my practice for a while. The toughest part's the oval shape in all its aspects. If I can get my time down to four seconds or under, it's going to simplify the operation greatly.

'And, by the way, Bernie. I wired Croesus in California, to tell him that the second switch is poised and ready to begin. Oswald Zec, who has been living in Paris and looking after Croesus's interests here ever since the *Mona Lisa* switch, will no doubt be monitoring the operation as before—and providing any help that's needed.'

Bernard Fosdyke stared at his accomplice in some surprise and not a little alarm.

'You mean we're going to double-cross the Nazis?' he asked. 'Is that—wise?'

'We'll double-cross them—and get away with it, Bernie,' said the other. 'The means by which we achieve the latter, I leave to your fecund brain. But one thing's for sure: those bastards are going to lay their sticky fingers on Leonardo's *Virgin* over my dead body.'

Fosdyke thought that over for a few moments, and felt constrained to add: 'And mine, Hal.' But he felt his flesh creep as he did so.

The letter written and posted along with the enclosure, and Hal Levy having got his time down to a whisker over four seconds per side plate, the two comrades voted unanimously to repair to the homely little restaurant that specialized in tête de veau; there they were greeted with no great show of enthusiasm by madame, who once again hustled the professor out of his seat to accommodate the newcomers at a table for two, provided them with an opened bottle of the house red wine unbidden, and went to stir the huge vat in which simmered the staple dish of the establishment.

Fosdyke poured a brimming glass of wine for each of them. 'To revert to the Nazis, Hal,' he said quietly. 'Is it your opinion that it was they who shot the policemen—and in mistake for us?'

'The idea took root last night,' replied the other, 'and has with some reluctance grown on me. Yes, I think you have it right.'

'They're a bad lot,' said Fosdyke, 'and they clearly mean business. Would it be a presumption on my part to ask how you chanced to incur their hatred and contempt to such a degree? They took an awful lot of time and trouble—not to mention risk—in pursuing you to a foreign country for the purpose of killing you. And all for the comparatively picayune sum of ten thousand marks. To me, this seems—out of all proportion.'

'The people we are dealing with, Bernie,' said the other, 'have no sense of proportion. This is an elegance they despise in others and consciously quench in themselves. The guy I gypped out of ten grand—he whom our friend with the windowpane stuck in his eye refers to as his "principal"—is a megalomaniac of the first order, whose self-esteem would be severely punctured if a newsboy on a street corner successfully palmed him short change for a quarter. For settling an account of the magnitude in question, he would have sent his lackeys to hound me over the face of the earth. However, since I intend to dispose of my various identities —including my true identity of Harold Hiram Levy—when this present operation is completed, his rancour is doomed to be unrequited.'

'I expect it would be prudent of me to do the same,' said Fosdyke. 'Change my identity, I mean.'

'Half a million bucks is a tremendous help in this regard,' said Levy. 'There's little that can assist a guy to fade into the background like half a million bucks. With that kind of dough, he can pull up the drawbridge, lower the portcullis, shut himself in his ivory tower and cock a snook at the world. Or, like your hero Murdoch, he could buy himself a paradise island in the South Seas and cock his snook from there.'

'Mmm, that's worth thinking about,' said Fosdyke. And he thought about it for a while—till he came to the part where a tiny but shapely figure came running up from the rolling surf to greet him, and she turned out to be Dorothy Batthyány. Then he pulled himself together.

Madame brought the two steaming dishes piled high with the glutinous stew of calves' cheek in cream sauce with mixed vegetables. Through the rising cloud of mouth-watering steam, Fosdyke looked up to see two uncomely faces staring wistfully at them through the window.

Levy had seen them, too.

'Amos 'n' Andy are going to take some shaking off,' he observed. 'But, like I said, that's going to be your department, Bernie.'

Charles Hyacinthe de Courcey (it was upon his wife's dictate that he had adopted the noble prefix 'de' in the interests of furthering his social and professional career) arrived at his office in the Louvre museum five minutes after the cleaners had departed, five minutes before his secretary was due, and well in advance of the morning's mail.

Safe in his commodious office, with its portraits of past Directors frowning down from their gilded frames all round the walls, de Courcey took off his overcoat and hat, kicked off his galoshes and invested his ankles with dove-grey spats, smoothed down his patent leather hair in the mirror, flicked up the ends of his handsome moustache, shook a little eau de Cologne on his hands and a dab behind his ears, admired himself in a pier glass from the tip of his shiny black hair to his patent leather shoes, taking in the tight-waisted black suit coat and striped pants, the faultlessly folded grey and white-speckled cravat, and the sprigged silk vest en route —and addressed himself to the tasks of the day.

The first task—and infinitely the most important—was the morning's mail. With every day of his Temporary and Acting appointment as Director of the Louvre museum pending the nomination of a permanent incumbent, de Courcey died a little with the arrival of the mail lest another day would go past and still no letter from the Ministry informing him that his appointment had been translated to a permanency; or, even worse, that a missive with the same letterhead would arrive to let him know that he could expect the new man to take up his post on such and such a date, and would M. de Courcey kindly extend to the new Director such assistance as lay within his power? Et cetera, et cetera.

Every morning, at the stroke of nine, the secretary, Mlle Lebrun, tapped on the door and was bidden to enter. It was the same on this particular day:

Tap-tap.

'Enter!'

Mlle Lebrun came in, holding to her spinsterish and vestigial bosom a wire tray containing the day's effusion. Sketching what approximated to a curtsy, she waited to hear what her lord and master required of her. Mlle Lebrun, who attended the cinema six evenings a week and was a devotee of Hollywood romances, in particular those starring Misses Norma Shearer and Kay Francis, Messrs George Brent and Frederic March, knew enough about the nuts and bolts of romantic love to know that she was besotted with Charles Hyacinthe de Courcey.

'That will be all, thank you, mam'selle,' said de Courcey, whose eye, having no attraction towards the minuscule charms of the secretary, was already scanning the raft of envelopes, seeking to find the one that had the size and shape and luxurious thickness that betokened the expensive stationery of the Ministry.

Mlle Lebrun sketched another curtsy and departed to have a good cry in the staff ladies' powder room.

Half to his chagrin, half to his relief, de Courcey registered the fact that there was no communication, for good or ill, from the powers that be, and was about to telephone his wife Marie-Claire to that effect (she waited by the instrument every morning at that hour and could not bring herself even to clean her teeth, let alone shrug off her wrapper, do her hair, put on make-up—till she had heard the news, be it good, bad, or nothing), when something prompted him first to open that part of the mail which was not discernibly composed of brochures and circulars. In so doing, it might be said that he greatly advanced the cause of Messrs Fosdyke and Levy.

The missive from the latter pair was almost the first he opened and he read both the introductory letter and its enclosure with considerable interest and some puzzlement. It has to be said that it was the collection of the notoriously well-known signatures at the foot of the latter sheet which prompted him to connect with his wife immediately.

' 'Allo?'

'Marie-Claire, dearest heart . . .'

'Hyacinthe! Is there any news? Tell me, before I faint away!'

'No news from the Ministry, my angel—but a very curious thing . . .'

'Tell me, tell me! Don't say that you have had an offer of an assistant directorship in some backwater of the Car-margue, or wherever! I may as well tell you now, Hyacinthe, that you need not look to me for support if you were to acccept such an insulting offer.'

'No, no, my treasure—this is an offer from a prominent English savant and his associate. They want the Louvre to collaborate in an artistic enterprise—to which end, they have invited me to a working dinner at the Tour d'Argent. Now—what do you think of that?'

'I confess myself impressed, Hyacinthe. The Tour d'Argent always has a very sincere ring and commands immediate respect in the breast. But what of the bona fides of your proposed hosts?'

He told her of the signatures endorsing the letter of introduction, and her voice rose by nearly half an octave.

'But this is wonderful, Hyacinthe! You must know that the Stein woman is fabulously rich and influential, and Jean Cocteau is received in the highest circles. I am not so sure of the rest, and have been told that the Ministry is pledged to perpetuity that none of Signor Picasso's daubs will ever see the inside of the Louvre—but he is, nevertheless, a painter of international standing. This English savant and his associate mix in very heady circles. In your position, my dearest Hyacinthe, you cannot afford to do other than embrace their invitation with both hands. When is this working dinner to be?'

'They offer Monday, Tuesday or Wednesday of next week, my precious.'

'Make it Monday—strike while the iron is hot. By Tuesday, you could be out of a job.'

De Courcey shuddered. 'Yes, dear. They propose to call at my office at six. I will obtain some whisky—the English like whisky—and have some petits fours brought in from Fauchon's.'

'Petits fours and whisky! How you do betray your petty bourgeois origins, Hyacinthe! You will serve champagne of the finest vintage. And caviar. Ikra caviar. Oh, you be- nighted creature! Where would you be without me?'

De Courcey, who in his more reflective moments had a pretty good idea where he might have been but for his wife, made no reply to this; but when she suggested that she might also invite herself to the dinner at the Tour d'Argent, he had enough fortitude to register a veto.

It was very much a morning for telephoning. The Herr Rittmeister, mindful that he and his minions had yet to carry out the order to 'eliminate' the scoundrel who had had the effrontery to defraud his 'principal' of ten thousand marks, put through a long-distance call to the latter's office in the Berlin Reichstag.

'Excellency, I am speaking from Paris.'

'Is the job done? The answer must be "yes"—none other is acceptable.'

'Excellency, I have good news. In order, as he thinks, to save his skin, the person in question is obtaining for you an authentic and original work which, for security's sake, I may not even hint at over the telephone. The acquisition, as you will appreciate when you see it, is—*colossal!*'

'You are a good man, Herr Rittmeister. A reliable officer.'

'I like to think, Excellency, that I continue to be the staunch follower that I was in the days when I flew as your wing-man in the Richthofen squadron.'

'You are, you are! But listen, when you have obtained this —this authentic and original work—the person in question, this scoundrel . . .'

'No names, Excellency, I beg you!'

'This scoundrel is to be *suitably repaid*. Understood?'

'Correct, Excellency. We understand each other perfectly.'

Then there began what, for the two conspirators, was an interminable weekend.

It began well: the reply to their invitation was brought round the following morning by messenger. It merely stated that the writer accepted with much pleasure the kind offer of a working dinner, to which the writer looked forward with happy anticipation, et cetera, et cetera.

Levy broke off from his painting exercises to join Fosdyke in an English breakfast of fried eggs and bacon, with sausages, grilled tomatoes, sauté potatoes, toast and marmalade and coffee. All around them, as they ate, the walls bore evidence of the artist's dedication: there was scarcely space on three sides in which to cram one more side plate, or another upright with a crosspiece. In addition, Levy had introduced a new exercise, which was hastily to obliterate a pencilled outline of irregular shape with what he described as a 'scumble'—that's to say he dashed across it several successive dark tones with a large and heavily-laden brush till the outline was gone. This took him no time at all.

'I'll continue with the good work,' said Levy, 'while you carry out the next part of the plan. Is there anything else we've forgotten?'

Fosdyke consulted a notebook that lay on the table beside his plate.

'Let's see,' he said. 'Stage one—complete. Stage two—complete. Stage three—acceptance of the invitation—complete.' He drew a neat pencil line through the latter item. 'Stage four—Secure Accommodation. That's my baby.'

'Be sure,' said Levy, 'not to stint yourself as to cost. We can dismiss it as temporary accommodation pending the setting-up of our regular studio-laboratory in Paris, but the joint must have the feel, the timbre—know what I mean? —of comfortable means and high scholarship lightly borne. I would suggest, if you can find any, the sort of highly uncomfortable leather armchairs much favoured in gentlemen's clubs in the St James's district of London: well worn, but worn well. You can also take a couple of my fake pictures: there's a tolerable oil sketch by Sisley over there—' pointing—'and an undoubted Boudin of the beach at Trouville. The Carot river scene is very fine, also. But maybe we should not overdo the scene-setting. What have I missed?'

'I have it all here,' said Fosdyke. 'Of course, we require ample storage space and—most importantly—a telephone in the lobby.'

'The latter,' said Levy, 'is the most vital item of all.'

Leaving his accomplice to his exercises, Fosdyke set out to find first-floor accommodation within a short walking distance of the Louvre. This was not difficult. He discovered a suite of two rooms and the usual offices above a shop in the Rue de Rivoli, not five minutes' walk from the entrance to the Louvre museum, with its own private entrance, a phone in the hallway, and running hot and cold water. The letting agent, upon receipt of a month's rent in advance, handed over the keys, and Fosdyke set to work to turn the accommodation into a place with the feel—in his accomplice's happy phrase—'of comfortable means and high scholarship lightly borne'. He took a cab to the flea market, where he found and purchased a pair of leather armchairs that must surely have emigrated from the veritable St James's, and even bore upon their headrests the darker imprint of generations of macassared heads, and upon the arms the tiny burn holes of red hot cigar fragments uncounted. He had these delivered to the Rue de Rivoli, along with a solid-looking walnut table of considerable dimensions, two straight-backed wooden chairs and a white-painted table to act as a sort of workbench.

In a photographic emporium, he bought a second-hand plate camera that was in need of some repair before it could be used, a plate enlarger in similar state, and an infra-red lamp that actually worked.

Late on the afternoon of that day, with the furnishings all delivered, he disposed them about the main room in an imaginative manner, afterwards standing well back to receive the effect he had contrived to create.

Something was missing, and he fingered it upon the instant: books. The room, with its air of scholarship lightly borne, needed a row of solid-looking volumes. It was approaching dusk, but he reckoned that he just about had time to catch the booksellers along the Quai du Louvre before the shut up their cabinets.

He had not walked far, and was seeking to cross the road between the plunging traffic of the Rue de Rivoli, when he saw—*her!*

She was sitting in the front passenger seat of a large and potent-looking Mercedes gran turismo. There was a man at the wheel: a soft-jowled, well-barbered man of middle age. Dorothy was laughing up into his face, and he was smirking with tight-lipped amusement at something she was saying.

Then she had gone past.

Fosdyke, throwing aside all thought of why and how, gave chase. When he found himself impeded by the strollers on the pavement, he ran out into the gutter, and was nearly brought under the wheels of a passing motor bus. Drivers opened their windows and threw curses at his unheeding ears. His whole being was directed towards the Mercedes, which was moving at a fair pace in the heavy traffic, but looked vulnerable to any check in its onward progress—as, for instance, at a junction.

Heart pounding, breath sobbing—for Fosdyke was by no means used to violent physical exercise—he maintained the same distance from the Mercedes, and might even have been gaining slightly, when, to his savage delight, the line of traffic was halted by a policeman with a white truncheon and a whistle. Fosdyke redoubled his efforts; dragged from out of his unfit frame and his unaccustomed heart, lungs and guts the fortitude to increase his pace, lest he should lose what would surely be his last chance to reach her.

He was within two cars' length of his quarry, and had already reached out a hand to grab—anything—when the policeman blew his whistle, waved his white truncheon, and the line of traffic moved on again, the Mercedes leading. It soon swept out of sight and was lost to him.

Fosdyke stood there in the gutter, with the noise of the passing charivari dinning in his ears, and the dull feeling of an irremediable deprivation.

CHAPTER 9

If Levy noticed any further quenching of his companion's spirits over the weekend, he made no comment; and when taken to see the newly-furbished accommodation, was full of praise for Fosdyke's enterprise and imagination. The place, with its furnishings and equipment, pictures, leather-bound books with impressively arcane titles and all, admirably lived up to their dictum.

On Sunday evening, they went to the cinema in the

Champs Elysées to see *Queen Christina*, starring the sensational Greta Garbo. Afterwards, they slipped over to the Left Bank and tackled yet another meal of Madame's tête de veau. And were followed there by their German shadows.

'Tomorrow at dawn,' declared Levy, 'we go "over the top". Are you scared?'

Fosdyke grinned and shrugged. 'A bit,' he confessed.

'Decided what you're going to do with your half-million?'

'No. Have you?'

'No.'

And there the conversation languished.

Monday morning dawned with an unexpected flurry of snow, which Levy applauded, because it would greatly assist their plan. In the previous week, on and off, they had added to the sum of knowledge about the comings and goings in the Louvre museum that Levy and his previous partner had garnered during the *Mona Lisa* switch. For instance, due to the changeable weather (the previous coup had taken place in a particularly equable high summer), they found that the attendance in the picture galleries was closely related to the state of the sky. If it was sunny, the folks stayed away, similarly if it snowed. One thing above all brought them in droves—and that was rain.

'If the snow keeps on,' said Levy, 'the goddamned place will be nearly empty till closing time.'

'So let's go.'

With the feelings of soldiers mounting an assault, or of conquistadors climbing the last mountain pass that must lead them to El Dorado, they walked through the swirling snowflakes with hearts held high and their fears well in check, arriving at the door of the museum two minutes after opening time.

'First attempt, Bernie,' said Levy, holding out his hand. 'Here's luck to us both. There's none like us.'

Fosdyke took the proffered hand. 'I've only one nagging

doubt, Hal,' he said, 'and it's that someone might notice between now and the time the gallery closes. I'm afraid I never took that into account when I was making the plan.'

'I did, Bernie,' said the other, 'and totally discounted it. I can't argue the psychology, for I'm not Nat Willis—but I can tell you categorically that the kind of folks who go rubbernecking in the Louvre on a snowy day in early February don't have the scholarship, nor indeed the real interest, to notice any such thing.'

With this cryptic assurance from Levy, the two parted company and went on into the museum, Fosdyke leading.

The adjacent galleries containing paintings of the Florentine School were watched over by the usual uniformed attendants with whom Fosdyke and Levy had familiarized themselves from afar, together with their comings and goings. As usual, when approaching the scene of their activities, both conspirators assumed superficial disguises: Levy a beret, a voluminous woollen scarf, and a pair of thick-rimmed library glasses; Fosdyke removed his cap and stuffed it in his pocket, and applied a false 'toothbrush-style' moustache under his nose. It was in this persona that he approached the attendant nearest to *The Virgin of the Rocks* and questioned him as to the whereabouts of the *Mona Lisa*.

The functionary, after a brief glance towards the only occupant of the gallery—a short-sighted personage in a beret who was standing in front of a picture by a Florentine artist of the second rank that was hung next but one to the *Virgin,* and assiduously scribbling in a notebook—consented to guide the disguised Fosdyke to the most famous picture in the Louvre, if not the world. This done, he was pleased to answer a couple of ludicrously banal questions relating to the subject of the portrait before returning to his post at the archway joining the two galleries. The whole evolution had taken thirty seconds by Fosdyke's watch. The attendant passed the scholarly individual on his way out, and Levy gave his fellow-conspirator an assured wink as he went on his way.

They met five minutes later in the courtyard outside. It was still snowing.

'How did it go, Hal?' asked Fosdyke.

'Like a charm,' replied the other. 'Give me another half-minute when the next shift of attendants takes over, and the job's done. Let's go and avail ourselves of a drink.'

They went to a café off the Rue de Rivoli, and Levy, producing his gunmetal cigar case, proceeded to mix a darker set of tints than the pale ochre that already occupied the makeshift, portable palette. This he did with a large camelhair brush—one of the set of brushes that he carried in the breast pocket of his overcoat.

'This will fix the last—and easiest—part of the job,' he said.

'Are you sure you should be drinking Scotch?' asked Fosdyke with a distinct note of peevishness, brought on by nerves, as the waiter set their order before them.

'In common with many of my calling,' replied Levy, 'I paint better and with a steadier hand when I have had one or two. Never fear—in a very short time from now, the job will have been done to our complete satisfaction, and all will be in readiness for the great switch!'

And so it proved to be.

They took a long time to get ready that afternoon. Both bathed in the unpromising hip bath that Levy produced from somewhere, and had to be filled from kettles of water heated on the gas ring. With only one reasonable suit to his name—and that going shiny at the knees and elbows and threadbare at the cuffs—Fosdyke was grateful to be provided with a tuxedo off the peg, together with a starched shirt, collar and bow tie—all paid for by Levy out of the 'capital fund'.

By half past five they were ready for their assignation with the Temporary Acting Director of the Louvre Museum

—and, incidentally, with Fate: Fosdyke in his tuxedo; Levy
in a more soigné attire of velvet smoking jacket and matching
pants, with his usual red carnation in the buttonhole. Questioned by his accomplice how he always contrived to obtain
such a bloom—even one of the hothouse sort—at that time
of the year, Levy confided that, when pushed, he was not
averse to wearing an artificial carnation made of silk; but
he simply didn't feel dressed, on formal occasions, without
a buttonhole of his favourite flower.

On the stroke of six o'clock, they presented themselves at
the door of the Louvre and rang the bell. They were admitted
by Mlle Lebrun, who had put on her prettiest frock for the
occasion. She smilingly led them to the office of the Director
and announced them, afterwards making herself scarce—
to their considerable relief.

'Ah!—Dr Fosdyke and Mr Levy. How do you do? Shall we
converse in English—yes?'

'As you please, sir,' replied Fosdyke, taking the Director's
proffered hand. 'Though both my associate and I speak
tolerable French.'

'Let it be English,' said de Courcey, who, from his fussily
ingratiating manner, had clearly swallowed their bait, hook,
line and sinker and was going to cooperate with whatever
proposals they put forward—always supposing that such
proposals were of benefit to the career of Charles Hyacinthe
de Courcey.

Now he was at the drinks table. 'I can only offer champagne,' he informed them. 'Krug '31—not the best year in
the calendar, I'm afraid.' So modest. So self-deprecating, it
wasn't true. 'And caviar,' he added, presenting a dish. 'A
nibble of Ikra won't spoil our appetites for dinner. Or a
cigar, perhaps?'

The silver box in which he presented the veritable tor-
pedoes among cigars bore on the underside of the lid—where
it could clearly be read by the presentee—an oleaginous

inscription that constrained the two conspirators to exchange straight-faced glances:

A notre chèr M. Charles Hyacinthe de Courcey
de ses collègues et amis dévoués
du Musée de Licq-Athérey (B.-Pyr.)
Le 20ième novembre, 1932
'Au revoir, cher Maître! Reviendrez!'

'A small tribute from the staff of my former gallery,' purred de Courcey, quite mistaking the significance of their glances.

'Charming,' murmured Fosdyke.

'Your health, gentlemen,' said their host, raising his glass. 'I am agog to hear the details of your enterprise. "Of considerable cultural and prestigious benefit to all parties" —that has a most seductive ring. Might one ask—and so early in our discussions—what is the basic premise of your proposition?'

'Most certainly, sir,' replied Fosdyke, and to his companion: 'I think we can show our hand thus far with discretion, don't you, my dear chap?'

'Oh yes indeed,' answered Levy. 'Should the proposition not be acceptable to the Louvre—supposing, for instance, that we are obliged to approach the National Gallery, London—or even the Uffizi, Florence—I'm sure we can rely upon M. de Courcey's discretion until we have made our arrangements.'

'Oh yes, gentlemen—yes!' breathed the Director with a fervour and sincerity that was moist-eyed with intensity. 'Oh, you may be sure that you can rely on my absolute discretion. But I hope and trust, gentlemen, that you will not find it necessary to approach the other galleries that you mention. I hope that the arrangement—whatever it is— may rest between ourselves.'

The bogus doctor of philosophy took another sip of his

champagne. 'There surely should be no impediment,' he opined, 'since our proposition will be of tremendous value to the Louvre, if only—to put it at its base commercial level . . .' He sniffed with distaste and made a moue.

'Commerce—*pah!*' interjected de Courcey, and pricked up his ears with a heightened interest.

'Unfortunately, it must be taken into account,' said Fosdyke. 'My colleague and I have estimated that your take at the turnstiles will be more than quadrupled as a result of this arrangement. However, set against that base commercialism, there is the critical and cultural esteem which will accrue to the gallery.'

'Oh, yes—most important, most important,' said de Courcey, looking positively radiant with delicious expectation. 'But what, pray, will be the—er—inducement for this happy state of affairs?'

It was Levy who answered. 'We have persuaded the private owners of no less than sixty Old Master paintings of the highest excellence and impeccable provenance, none of which has been shown publicly in the last hundred years and more, to be loaned to the Louvre—or to some other national institution of our choice—totally free of charge. For exhibition over a three-month period.'

If de Courcey had been holding his champagne glass at the time he must surely have dropped it. As it was, he could only stand and stare.

'Su-sixty?' he breathed. 'And fu-free of charge—for three months?'

'The owners—all of them persons to whom money means nothing,' said Fosdyke, 'seek only the warmth of public esteem and the envy of their peers.'

'They're even willing to foot the bill for the insurance,' added Levy.

The hand that took hold of the magnum of Krug '31 discernibly trembled with a most profound emotion as the Temporary Acting Director of the Louvre replenished their glasses. 'But this is wonderful, gentlemen—*wonderful!*' he cried.

'It was I who decided upon the Louvre as the venue for the exhibition,' said Fosdyke, 'though in fact it is many years since I last saw the arrangements here. Not since I was a student in 'nineteen. Many improvements must have been made in the years between.'

'Oh yes, they have, they have,' said de Courcey.

'I must look round the galleries at an early date,' said Fosdyke.

'You shall, you shall,' trilled de Courcey. 'Any time you please, my dear Doctor.'

The two conspirators exchanged sharp glances, and Fosdyke gave his companion a firm nod of the head.

'You'd hardly believe it,' said Levy, with a distinct touch of the wistful, 'but the way my life has unfolded, I have never before entered the Louvre, or seen the picture galleries.' He looked sadly into his drink.

De Courcey gave a start. 'Ah, my dear Mr Levy, dear Doctor Fosdyke, what am I thinking of?' he cried. 'What better time than now, when we have the place entirely to ourselves, for me to walk you through our tremendous display? Er—we do have some time before dinner, do we not?' he added anxiously.

'Over an hour and a half,' said Fosdyke. 'I ordered a table at the Tour d'Argent for eight.'

'Then let us go,' said de Courcey, 'and take our champagne with us!' So saying, he picked up the bottle and, tucking it under one arm with a playful wink, opened the door to his companions, who filed out, glasses in hands.

Both conspirators were smiling broadly.

They admired the Winged Victory of Samothrace, whose tremendous shape dominated the head of the great staircase. They rhapsodized over the seventeenth-century French masterpieces of Claude Lorrain and the obscure mysteries of Poussin. The collection of Dutch landscapes left Fosdyke a little cool, and the ever-sycophantic de Courcey could not but agree with him that there was something basically *commercial* about Dutch seventeenth-century painting in general—'Almost as if, my dear Doctor, it had been priced by the yard, haha." They progressed through the Italian section by way of the primitive to the Siennese and on to the School of Florence—and it was there, declared Harold Hiram Levy, that his true interests lay.

They came at length to the *Mona Lisa*, and de Courcey waxed proprietorial about the most famous painting in the world, one might have thought that he had executed it himself, while—supreme irony!—the true begetter stood watching and listening with his head on one side and a quiet smile on his lips.

A little further along, in the adjoining gallery . . .

'May I now present,' said de Courcey with the air of a man introducing a paradox, '*The Virgin of the Rocks!*' He smiled from one to another of them. After a few moments of silence, his smile faded at the edges.

'Gentlemen, is—is something the *matter?*' he breathed.

Fosdyke looked puzzled. 'Levy, do you see what I see?' he asked.

'Most odd!' replied the other. 'I wonder . . .'

'Gentlemen, gentlemen,' said de Courcey, and a note of real anxiety had entered his voice. 'What are you trying to *say?*'

Fosdyke laughed shortly. 'Ah, my dear de Courcey,' he said, wagging a finger, 'you are testing and trying us, but Levy and I were not born yesterday, haha.'

'Indeed not,' contributed Levy. 'But it was a most interesting attempt. Confess it now, monsieur—you have made an exchange. Yes?'

'An—*exchange?*' breathed de Courcey. 'Wha-what do you mean?'

'Why, monsieur,' said Levy, still banteringly amused,

'you must know that this is not the Louvre version of the *Virgin.*'

'It—it is *not?*' whispered de Courcey.

'No, no,' interposed Fosdyke. 'This is the National Gallery, London version. There are many differences, large and small, but of course the haloes above the heads of the Virgin and the infants spring most readily to the eye—' he gestured over the painting with his open hand—'together with the staff and cross that rests on the infant John the Baptist's shoulder. None of these are in the Louvre version . . .'

'But *your* version has the angel pointing towards the Baptist,' supplied Levy. 'And there is no such hand in this picture.'

De Courcey made no reply; he could only stand (and barely so) and slowly shake his head, as if trying to will his two companions to go away.

'Own up, my dear de Courcey,' said Fosdyke banteringly. 'Either this is the version from the National Gallery, with whom you have no doubt arranged a temporary exchange . . .'

'Or it is a copy of the same,' supplied Levy. 'In short— a fake.'

'A—*a fake?*'

The Temporary Acting Director of the Louvre Museum fainted on his feet, and would have fallen if they had not caught him.

They half-dragged, half-carried the wretched man back down to his office and shut the door. By chafing his hands and feeding him sips of champagne, they presently brought him to a state that approximated to normalcy. The total moral collapse of Charles Hyacinthe de Courcey was not far distant, though he still had a few querulous objections to raise.

'It can't be true!' he wailed. 'I believe that, some years ago, an attempt was made to steal the *Mona Lisa*—a most audacious attempt—but the thieves concerned were unable to get the picture any further than the street door. How could anyone possibly have—*exchanged*—a painting the size of *The Virgin of the Rocks?*'

'The question is,' said Levy, 'when was the exchange effected? Assuming that an exchange took place, why has no one noticed it before? The attendants, for instance? Yourself, monsieur?'

The attendants and their merits de Courcey dismissed with a contemptuous shrug. As to himself, well . . .

Well, they deduced, he seldom went near the picture galleries, being essentially an administrator, a civil servant. They elicited that he scarcely knew of the existence of the London version of the *Virgin*. But he rummaged in a filing cabinet and produced a catalogue raisonné of the National Gallery which contained small monochrome reproductions of the principal possessions, including the masterpiece in question. Upon gazing at it, de Courcey uttered a small groan. There, clearly to be seen, were the haloes, the staff and the cross, the absence of the angel's pointing hand.

By now, Fosdyke and Levy had long abandoned their simulated attitude of having been the objects of a prank on de Courcey's part, and seemed in deadly earnest.

'Let us examine the alternatives,' said Levy. 'One: some person, or persons, has stolen the original and substituted a copy—a very excellent copy—of the National Gallery version, perhaps because he had such a picture already in his possession. Two: the picture upstairs is *indeed* the National Gallery version (and I think we can discount that). Three: your version has been deliberately tampered with for some reason or another. Perhaps to discredit you, de Courcey.' He looked long and hard at the wretched man. 'Do you have any enemies who might wish to destroy your career, monsieur?'

It was then that de Courcey's nerve broke . . .

'I am surrounded by enemies who wish me ill!' he cried,

his voice rising to a note of hysteria. 'The people in the gallery here. The Keeper of Pictures. The Keeper of Sculpture. The Archivist. All of them. They're all after my job. And the attendants—they all hate me and resent me.' His expression took on a mask of cunning. 'And there are the people at the Ministry. They don't know that I know they're plotting against me, to bring in a nobody to be the permanent Director. But I know—ah yes, I know! They want to get me back to the provinces. And now they'll achieve their end!' He pointed a shaking finger to the cigar box, its lid open to show the fawning inscription. 'When the story of this comes out, *I shall be sent back to that hell-hole!*'

Stung to compassion, Fosdyke reached out a hand to lay on the wretched man's arm. 'My dear de Courcey,' he said, 'I'm sure we can contrive . . .'

'And *she* won't come with me!' cried de Courcey. '*That bitch of a wife of mine will leave me!*'

It was at this poignant moment that the door sprang open, and Mlle Lebrun stood on the threshold, looking rather like a scaled-down Amazon queen contemplating a field of her slaughtered followers. Her vestigial bosom rose and fell in deep emotion. She had lost some hairpins, and one side of her coiffure had fallen. Her eyes blazed.

'Don't worry, Hyacinthe!' she cried. '*I* shall never leave you, my darling!' And, advancing into the room, she embraced the astounded de Courcey. 'Lay your poor tired head on my breast,' she murmured. 'Joséphine will succour you.'

Levy and Fosdyke exchanged horrified glances; while the advent of his secretary, together with her astonishing display, seemed to rally de Courcey, he shook her off—none too gently—and addressed the others in a calmer tone of voice.

'Enough of this,' he said. 'I have listened to your reasoning, gentlemen, and it makes good sense to me. Dr Fosdyke was about to say, before I rudely interrupted him, that something could be contrived. What, pray, might be contrived, to save *The Virgin of the Rocks*—and, incidentally, my reputation?'

'Oh, do but listen to him!' cried Mlle Lebrun. 'What calm majesty! Such forcefulness!'

'I think,' said Fosdyke, 'that we must subject the painting upstairs to scientific examination; first, to determine if it is indeed by the hand of Leonardo; secondly, to decide which of the two versions is presently in your possession. The question of whether it is the Louvre version and has been tampered with in some way will emerge in the examination.'

'I must have those answers!' snapped de Courcey. 'But how—and where—is this examination to be carried out? Tell me that, gentlemen.'

'What command!' trilled Mlle Lebrun. 'What presence! A second Napoleon!'

'It can be done in our laboratory-studio,' replied Fosdyke, 'which is only a stone's throw from here.'

'And how long will it take, Doctor?'

'An hour—less.'

'You mean—in an hour, I shall know all the anwers? Then let it be done, my friend.'

'I will accompany you, Hyacinthe!' cried Mlle Lebrun. 'We will face the truth together, for good or ill.'

'We will do no such thing!' snapped de Courcey. 'You stay where you are. And don't answer the telephone!'

Mlle Lebrun backed away against the wall, a great glory in her eyes, her bosom rising and falling with passion unleashed—unleashed, yet brought to heel by the mastery of a strong-willed man.

Ten minutes later, the two conspirators and their willing and grateful victim were trudging through the snow and darkness, across the Louvre courtyard, towards the ad hoc establishment in the Rue de Rivoli. And with them they bore *The Virgin of the Rocks*.

*

Fosdyke had to admit to himself in all modesty, when he switched on the lights in the 'laboratory', that the place certainly exuded the 'tone' for which they had striven. The well-worn but worn well armchairs (to one of which they directed the still dazed but rallying de Courcey), the photographic gear—useless as it stood, but with the look of years of hard-nosed use and no nonsense. And the paintings.

They laid the *Virgin,* face uppermost, on the solid walnut table. Levy poured them all a liberal measure of Scotch. Fosdyke stooped over the picture and examined its smooth surface at close quarters through a magnifying-glass.

'If this brushwork is not by the hand of the supreme master himself,' he said, 'it is the most astonishing facsimile I have ever set eyes upon. Ah, but the infra-red exposure will betray the fraud—if fraud it is.'

'You cannot begin to imagine how grateful I am to you gentlemen for your timely assistance,' said de Courcey. 'And how providential your arrival in my hour of need.'

The two conspirators forbore to reply to that; Levy contented himself by topping up their glasses.

'I think we shall make the exposure, my dear Levy,' opined Fosdyke. Levy nodded.

They brought round the infra-red lamp on its standard, and, setting it so that the business end was directed downwards upon the painting, switched on. Immediately, the surface of the pigments was bathed in the unearthly light that made nonsense of their true colours.

'As you are no doubt aware, my dear de Courcey,' said Fosdyke, 'the system of photography by ultra-violet light has largely superseded the old system of the X-ray in probing out the layers of earlier work that invariably exist in fake Old Masters. It is a system both quicker and more efficient. Though, it has to be said, it requires a more profound knowledge of painting techniques.'

'What my colleague modestly forbears to point out,' interposed Levy, 'is that the infra-red system was devised by himself. And the system is becoming generally known in the art historicity profession as "Fosdyke's Method".'

'I do not cease to be grateful that, in my hour of need, I fell among men such as yourselves,' breathed de Courcey.

'Then I think we will . . .' began Fosdyke.

'Telephone!' said Levy, cocking an ear.

'I—um—hear no telephone,' said de Courcey; but Levy was already out of the door and shutting it behind him.

De Courcey watched as Fosdyke trundled the huge plate camera into place on its wheeled tripod, and directed it down upon the central section of the painting, in line with the heads of the figures. He then made a great play of setting the focus, sliding an unexposed plate into the rear of the apparatus, preparing for the moment of truth. He had just taken in hand the bulb that worked the shutter when Levy burst back into the room, his eyes alight with urgency.

'What is it, my dear fellow?' demanded Fosdyke.

'The secret's out—our secret's out!' cried the other. 'By tomorrow morning all Paris will know!'

'Ah, mon Dieu!' wailed de Courcey.

'Who was that on the telephone?' snapped Fosdyke.

'*Le Figaro*,' replied Levy. 'One of their readers was in the Louvre this afternoon. He phoned in and told the news desk that there was something very odd about the *Virgin*—and went on to tell them what!'

'I am ruined—*ruined*!' cried de Courcey, and burst into tears.

'Why did they get on to *us*?' demanded Fosdyke.

'They tried to reach M. de Courcey, but could get no reply from his office,' said Levy, 'so, knowing we were in town, they rang us—the experts.'

'What did you tell them—about the picture?'

'About the picture—nothing. But I told them that de Courcey was with us here. And they want to speak to him. They're still on the line.'

De Courcey shrank back in his seat and tried to make

himself look very small. 'No—no!' he breathed. 'I—I can't speak to them. What would I say? You—you, my friends, you speak to them for me.'

'Pull yourself together, man,' said Fosdyke. 'Only you can talk yourself out of this mess. That paper must be silenced. And it's entirely up to you.'

'But—but what shall I tell them? How shall I *explain* . . . ?'

Levy thought deeply for a few moments. Then, snapping finger and thumb, he cried: 'Admit everything!'

'*Everything?*' Both men stared at him in differing degrees of alarm.

'Well, nearly everything,' said Fosdyke. 'Tell them that Dr Fosdyke and Mr Harold Hiram Levy, the distinguished art experts, are in Paris to advise—among other things— upon the *Virgin*. Tell them—um—that Fosdyke and Levy are examining the picture under laboratory conditions to determine the degree of humidity that will be required to keep it in prime condition for yet another four hundred years.'

'And that they have lent you a very excellent copy of the London version from their own collection to hang in the gallery so as not to disappoint your visitors,' added Levy.

'Yes, that's it!' exclaimed Fosdyke. 'Away with you, de Courcey, old chap.'

Tearfully, pathetically, the Temporary Acting Director of the Louvre Museum spread his hands. 'What good will that *do* me, gentlemen?' he asked.

'It will buy you a little time,' said Levy. 'If they keep the story out of the paper tomorrow morning, and we get the answers tonight, you could be in the clear.'

De Courcey seemed to pull himself together. 'I will try it,' he said.

'Good man!'

'Away you go. And the best of luck!'

They watched him go and closed the door behind him.

As they busied themselves, they carried on a sporadic conversation:

'You timed that telephone call very well, Hal. Right at the critical moment.'

'And Oswald Zec was ready and waiting for me to ring him.'

'Hope he doesn't put too much of a scare into de Courcey. I thought, earlier on, that he was going to have a heart attack on us.'

'Mmmm. But I'm more concerned about the secretary bird,' said Levy. 'We hadn't bargained for the likes of her as a witness. By the time we've sewn de Courcey up the middle and nailed him to the ceiling, he won't speak a word of tonight's happenings, not even on his death bed. But the secretary bird—she's another case entirely.'

'We'll think of something to keep her quiet, Hal,' said Fosdyke. 'Hold everything—here comes de Courcey!'

The change in de Courcey's demeanour amply demonstrated the success of his telephone conversation. He was positively beaming.

'Well?' asked the conspirators, more or less in unison.

'It worked!' cried de Courcey. 'The news editor was most civil, most understanding. He said that, considering the circumstances, there was no story to print, and that it would indeed be a shame to spoil my visitors' delight by publishing the fact that the picture is spurious. He went on to liken the temporary exchange to when a famous actor is indisposed and a talented understudy takes over his role for a performance or two.'

'How very sympathetic of the news editor,' said Fosdyke. 'Truly, one comes across the nicest people in the most unexpected circumstances.'

'Well, then, my friends,' said de Courcey. 'How goes the examination? Do you have any news for me?'

Fosdyke looked at Levy; Levy looked at Fosdyke.

'Do you tell him—or should I?' asked the latter.

'I think it behoves you to break the good news, my dear Doctor,' said the other.

Fosdyke beamed. 'You have nothing to worry about, my dear de Courcey,' he said. 'As my colleague will now demonstrate!'

Grinning broadly, Levy absented himself for a minute and returned bearing a dripping cloth, which he proceeded to wipe over the painting as it lay upon the table.

'Aaaah! What are you doing?—Imbécile!' With a cry of anguish, de Courcey moved forward to strike aside Levy's sacrilegious hand, as, sweeping the damp cloth upon the surface of the picture, he released a mass of liquefied paint —umbers and various degrees of grey, black and darkly neutral colours, all mixing and snaking across the priceless images of the Madonna and her companions.

Fosdyke restrained the frantic man. 'Keep calm, my dear chap,' he said. 'All will be well. Wait—and watch.'

Having created a thoroughgoing mess upon the entire centre passage of the picture, Levy wrung out his cloth and, with a wink in de Courcey's direction, wiped it deftly across the slopping paint, soaking it up, bit by bit, puddle by puddle, till all was gone.

And there—plain to see, were the unsullied heads of the Virgin, the infant Jesus and John the Baptist, all without haloes and John without the slender staff and cross. And, last of all, there emerged the elegant, pointing hand of the winged angel.

'It—it's a miracle!' breathed de Courcey.

'A small miracle, perhaps,' conceded Fosdyke. 'It was the infra-red that showed up the answer to the riddle. You have been the victim of a cruel deception, my friend. Some joker has done a little—er—unauthorized extra work—upon your *Virgin*. Happily, he executed the embellishments in water-soluble gouache, and no harm is done. Nor would have been done—save, perhaps, to your professional reputation, for not having immediately spotted the transformation.

'I think you should pour M. de Courcey another Scotch, Levy. He is looking rather faint.'

CHAPTER 10

They carried *The Virgin of the Rocks* to the Louvre, to the wall which it was destined to grace till perpetuity; squelching through the snowbound night, with a bolt of canvas draped over the precious burden.

Into the great museum, up the staircase, past the Winged Victory of Samothrace, up into the galleries of the Florentine School. And Mlle Lebrun went too . . .

Mlle Lebrun was standing on the outside of the small group as they looked up and regarded the Madonna and her companions gathered among the cavernous rocks in the mysterious communion that the mind and heart of Leonardo da Vinci had devised. She—Mlle Lebrun—was now privy to the secret of the disfigured masterpiece, and rejoiced with her boss that, thanks to the brilliance of Fosdyke and Levy, he had been saved from disgrace, calumny and ruin. All the way up to the Florentine galleries she had hung upon de Courcey's arm, nor had his snappy attempts to shake her off and silence her endearments put her remotely out of countenance. As a fly is fixed forever in amber, the shocks of that astonishing evening had fixed her attitude to the man whom she had hitherto worshipped only from afar: his, now, was the mastery, and she his slave.

Fosdyke and Levy saw all this—if the same could not be said of the recipient, the loved one. And they grew uneasy.

'Well, my friends,' said de Courcey at length, gesturing for the umpteenth time at the picture. 'The nightmare is over. I wish it were possible for me to propose you for a suitable degree of the Légion d'Honneur, but it would not be either opportune or prudent. Perhaps on another occasion . . . '

'Thank you, monsieur,' replied Fosdyke, who had been exchanging meaningful glances and nods with his fellow-conspirator. 'Um—my colleague and I would like a last word with you before we close this part of the proceedings.' He glanced towards Mlle Lebrun, who was gazing seraphically at her adored one. 'Um—alone, if you please.'

'Of course,' responded de Courcey, and to the woman: 'Leave us, will you?'

'For you, dearest—anything,' she murmured, and kissed her hand to him. 'You'll find me down in your office, opening another magnum of champagne.' She giggled girlishly, turned on her heel and trotted away.

'I think that woman has gone mad,' observed de Courcey. 'Or is she merely drunk and incapable?'

'That broad,' said Levy—'sorry, that lady—is dangerous. Give it a week, or less, and she'll be telling the story of tonight's proceedings in any old bar on any old street corner.'

'He's right, you know,' said Fosdyke. 'She's a blab-mouth if I ever saw one.'

'Do not say so,' breathed de Courcey. 'But—what's to be done to silence her? I have a little money put aside . . .'

'You won't buy her with money,' said Levy flatly. 'There's only one way to shut her big mouth.' And, leaning forward, he whispered in de Courcey's ear.

'NO!' cried the Temporary Acting Director of the Louvre Museum. 'I would not do such a thing. My honour! The love that I bear my wife. And besides, gentlemen—you have *seen* the lady! Need I say more!'

'Aw, c'mon, man,' persisted Levy. 'You're a man of the world, a Frenchman furthermore. She's not grotesque, and she's got a loving heart. You'll be doing her a favour and ensuring your own future. On the other hand—take your chance. We've done all we can to save your skin.' He turned his back on de Courcey and motioned his companion to follow him out of the gallery.

'No, no—wait!' cried de Courcey.

'Yes?' They both paused.

'You think that she will keep silent if I—I *compromise*— her?'

'It will set the seal on the regard in which she holds you,' said Devy. 'And she will treasure the memory—and the man—all her life. When she is an old, old lady, it will warm her days and enrich her nights. She will also keep her big mouth shut about the picture.'

'I—I will do it!' cried de Courcey.

'Take her to the Tour d'Argent,' said Fosdyke. 'It's only half past nine and I've no doubt they've kept our table.'

They parted in the hallway outside de Courcey's office, and shook hands. No mention of the ostensible reason for their visit: the Temporary Acting Director of the Louvre Museum had had a most distracting evening, and there was more to follow.

They watched him walk towards the door of his office with the tread of a man approaching the scaffold. And then they left.

Back in their 'laboratory', they took from out of the capacious cupboard, where they had hidden it, the veritable *Virgin* from the Louvre and set the masterpiece up on a chair against a wall; then stood back and gazed upon it in rapture.

'She's ours,' Bernie,' breathed Levy. 'Against all reason and likelihood, we now own her.'

'A pity,' said Fosdyke, 'that we've got to let her go to Croesus. And just for a lousy million bucks.'

'What are you going to do with your half million, Bernie? Made up your mind yet?'

'Yes,' said Fosdyke, making it up upon the instant. 'For a start, I'm going to employ private detectives to find one

girl in all Paris. Then I'm going to ask her to marry me—
if she'll have me.'

'This is the girl you met when you were doing the survey?'

Fosdyke nodded, but didn't seem inclined to want to
pursue the matter further. So Levy said: 'Well, I guess we'd
better ring Zec and confirm that we've pulled off the job, so
that he can come round here and check it out as referee.'

'How can he possibly know that we haven't done a
double-cross on Croesus?' asked Fosdyke. 'This could be
your fake, and the real *Virgin* still in the Louvre. It would
certainly have simplified things for us.'

'That cunning bastard has his ways,' Levy assured his
companion. 'He'll know she's the real *Virgin*, right enough.'

Oswald Zec was feeling mightily pleased with himself. *The
Virgin of the Rocks* job sounded pretty okay. Levy would ring
up any time now and confirm that the heat was off—so's
he could go around and check the thing out for real. He was
a smart cookie, and it would take him only a couple of
seconds to know if the picture was one of Levy's fakes or
the genuine article. It was so simple: on Friday last, he had
gone to the gallery, and, when no one was about, he had
made a couple of tiny pin holes on the underside of the
picture frame. Easy!

Meanwhile, waiting for the call, he composed a letter to
his wife back in Detroit. Miriam, he stood convinced, was
cheating him with some guy, which was why she had stub-
bornly refused to join him in Paris save for the occasional
vacation, giving as her excuse that her old ma couldn't bear
to lose her. Leave it till Ma croaked, wrote Miriam many
times, and she would join him in Paree for good. To anticipate this happy conjunction of events, he had written to
Morrie the Breaks who had been the hit man with him in
the Weinburg gang before he went to work as fixer for The
Big Guy, and negotiated the untimely and painless removal
of Ma for two grand. And hadn't Morrie the Breaks written

back with the surprising information that Miriam's old lady
had shrugged off this mortal coil a year past?

Zec read over the letter again:

Dearest Miriam,

    I want for you to do me a small favor, which is to go
see Morrie the Breaks, who is living at 1615 West 23rd,
apartment three. Morrie has something to deliver to you
on my behalf . . .

'*Who's there?*' He looked up sharply from the letter, as the
door creaked open, and a silhouetted figure appeared with
the hall light behind him. 'Who the hell are you?' he challenged the newcomer.

No reply. The figure edged forward, slightly into the light
—so that the man at the table could see the pistol in the
other's hand. It had a potent-looking silencer screwed over
the muzzle, which made no more than the sound of a cork
being drawn when the trigger was pulled.

Before the killer's soft footsteps had faded down the stairs,
the telephone jangled out in the silent room, where the
man who had trusted nobody had departed to join his late
mother-in-law.

It rang out for quite a while, then stopped.

'That's goddamned odd,' said Levy, replacing the earpiece.

'No reply?' asked Fosdyke. 'But he was supposed to wait
for your call.'

'I don't like it,' said the other. 'When the good fairy was
handing out virtues, it's sure as hell Zec wasn't standing in
the front rank to receive. But one virtue he does have, and
that's constancy. That guy has the dedicated constancy of
a killer shark. So what could have happened to him?'

Another call ten minutes later, and yet another, still
brought no reply. Before Levy could try yet again, their own
telephone rang.

'So, Herr Henry Higgins—you have the merchandise, yes?'

'It's the Nazis,' said Levy, sotto voce, hand over the mouthpiece. 'Well, things aren't quite finalized yet,' he said to the man on the other end of the line.

'Do not try to pull the wool over my eyes, Herr Higgins, 'they have got the bells on,' came the reply. 'I know that you have made the exchange, because my men have followed you through every part of the operation. The merchandise is with you now at the place in the Rue de Rivoli—and we are coming to fetch it now. No tricks!'

The line went dead.

'Well?' queried Levy.

'They're on their way here. They'll pick up the *Virgin* and we'll get our pay-off.'

'Bullets in the back of the neck.'

'You bet! That guy's principal allowed his life member-ship of the League of Mercy to lapse while he was still in the cradle.'

'So we get out—and take the *Virgin* with us.'

'Right! Cover her over to keep out the chill night air, and let's go—out the back way!'

The windows to the rear of the ground floor were barred, but those of the floor above were not impeded. From there, the fall to the ground was no more than six feet when hanging by the hands from the window-sill. Fosdyke went first and found himself in a narrow, dark street. Levy lowered the *Virgin* to him on her own stout picture cord and then followed after. They bore their precious burden three blocks away from the Rue de Rivoli, till they came at length to an unlocked gate that led into a yard piled high with packing cases.

'Rest up here, Bernie,' said Levy. 'I'll go get the Rolls from the Left Bank and be back here right as soon as I can. It's for sure we've shaken off the Nazis. Our next trick will be to find some place to lie low till the heat's off.'

'And where will that be, Hal?'

The other grinned in the moonlight and patted his companion on the shoulder. 'Think it through,' he said. 'Where in all Paris can we draw upon a debt of gratitude and rest our tired old heads in peace?'

The cossetting luxury of the Tour d'Argent, the consummately practised attention of the platoon of waiters who responded to his every beck and call, together with the wine and spirits he had consumed, to say nothing of the swingeing shocks of the evening followed by the tremendous relief, had the effect of soothing de Courcey's highly-strung nerves to a quite remarkable degree. True, his dinner companion was not all he might have wished. Not a womanizer (he would, indeed, have been most assiduously uxorious if only his wife Marie-Claire had been the sort of woman to put up with his oily attentions), he nevertheless daydreamed of infidelity, but always with a female of a vastly different sort from Mlle Lebrun, with her unshapely frame, her mousey hair forever falling down, her desperate eagerness and—upon this evening of all evenings—her insane assumption of the role of his inamorata.

She was prattling on again, totally disregarding the exquisite dish of Croustade de Barbue 'Lagrené' which he had chosen for the fish course. And the subject—her subject—was *him*.

'I saw you from the first as Charlemagne, with the presence of Napoleon,' she gushed. 'And something of Bertrand du Guesclin, you know. Oh, dearest Hyacinthe, how I bless this evening.'

'This evening has been hell!' growled the object of her outpourings.

'For you—yes,' she conceded. 'But you rose above it like a flame. As for me—I have been emboldened to speak of the passion that you inspired in me from the first. Had it not been for you,' she added, 'I would have left the employ of the Louvre when my Uncle Joseph died.'

De Courcey, who had drunk enough, and was sufficiently irritated by his companion to be truculent, if not rude, growled in reply: 'And what the devil has the death of your damned Uncle Joseph to do with the matter?'

'Why,' she replied with a smile, unconscious—or uncaring—of his incivility, 'his legacy makes it quite unnecessary for me to go out to work.'

De Courcey laughed shortly. 'Humph!—your little *dot* wouldn't last you for long, young woman. You'd be back at work in a few months.' He would have added, 'And for the rest of your life—for all the hope *you* have of landing a husband,' but even he felt that to be rather too cutting.

'Oh no, Hyacinthe dearest,' she said demurely, pushing a morsel of brill around her plate with no great enthusiasm, 'I don't have to work again for the rest of my life, you know.'

De Courcey paused in the act of lifting a forkful to his lips.

'What did you say?' he demanded.

'The vineyard attached to the château produces enough to make ten thousand dozen bottles a year,' she said.

'The—er—vineyard?' he breathed.

'Yes, Hyacinthe. Three hundred prime hectares on the north bank of the Loire above Vouvray. The château overlooks it.'

'The château—ah . . .'

'Yes, that was given to Uncle Joseph's ancestor by St Louis.'

'St Louis—ah . . .'

'The king they made a saint, you know. Uncle Joseph's ancestor afterwards died of his wounds in the arms of the king during a Crusade.'

'During a Crusade—ah . . .'

'Yes.'

De Courcey reached out and, forestalling the hovering wine waiter, took from out of its silver bucket the bottle of

Dom Perignon that was chilling there. Somehow he found his voice, which had unaccountably become hoarse and breathless.

'More champagne, my dear—er—Joséphine,' he murmured.

It was chilly in the yard, and Fosdyke was constrained to march up and down—four paces one way and three the other—to prevent his feet from going to sleep. At every turn, he stopped and, lifting up the edge of the canvas, peered down and communicated with the *Virgin*—and she upside down at the time.

An hour and a quarter after his departure, the sweet purring of a decelerating Rolls-Royce engine announced the return of H. H. Levy.

'God, it took you long enough,' complained Fosdyke.

'I took the scenic route,' said the other. 'It occurred to me that when our Nazi friends found the little birds flown the nest, they might have thought to keep watch on the Concorde bridge—so I went by way of the Pont Neuf. Let's get our darling *Virgin* aboard.'

'Will she get in the Rolls?'

'Of course, dumb-bell—Rollses were specially designed with her in mind.'

In the event, *The Virgin of the Rocks* fitted into the rear section of the Silver Ghost with the hood down and a few inches to spare all round—discounting the back of Fosdyke's neck, where, seated in the front passenger seat, he received a rabbit punch from the edge of the frame when Levy took a sharp left-hand turn out of the narrow street.

As the Rolls's red rear lamp receded into the distance, the headlights of a large pantechnicon that had been parked near the entrance to the narrow street pulsed brightly. The engine started, and the man who had been patiently waiting and watching set off in pursuit.

*

'You've figured where we're going, Bernie?' asked Levy.

'To *La Ronde*,' replied Fosdyke. 'You're quite right. Having disposed of the bodies of those two crooked coppers, Madame can surely refuse us nothing in the way of shelter and comfort.'

'Add to that,' said Levy, 'the Nazis, at least, won't dare to set foot within a mile of the place in case one or other of them might be identified as being one of the guys who fired the shots. We'll lie low there, I propose, till we can raise Zec on the telephone. And I'm here to tell you, Bernie, that I am somewhat more than worried about Zec. His non-presence is so totally out of character that I am disposed to think he may have run into trouble.'

'What kind of trouble?' asked Fosdyke, puzzled.

'When a million dollars is concerned,' replied his companion, 'trouble follows as night follows day. You could even say that the essentially sincere sum of one million smackers is a positive lure for any kind of trouble that should happen to be snaking around.'

'Mmmm,' responded Fosdyke, assembling all the likely trouble that came to mind.

They came at last to the narrow, darkened street that housed their chosen sanctuary. Nothing had changed. The establishment in question was shuttered and locked. A rap on the door brought—in no great hurry—the eyes and nose of the epicene Loulou.

'Fermé!' declared Loulou firmly.

'You can't be closed to us,' declared Levy. 'We're friends of the house. Tell Madame we're here.'

The Judas window was closed, and the door was opened very soon afterwards. Mme Brunelleschi wafted towards them on an olfactory wave of scent and household enamel. She wore a coarse apron over a lace frock.

'My dear gentlemens!' she cried, embracing them both. 'We are closed to all but you. For this is our week for the painting and decorating. All the girls is at work. Voyez!'

'Bernard! Chéri!' Yvonne came running. She was in what Fosdyke knew from the clandestine perusal of certain magazines were called 'cami-knickers'. And this vestigial garment was augmented by a kitchen apron worn over the top, the latter abundantly splashed with pink paint. Flinging her arms round his neck, she proceeded to do disturbingly liquid things to his mouth, while he tried to think of his mother.

Levy, receiving similar ministrations from two other girls —also attired as for painting in a bordello—and presently contriving to free himself, replied to Mme Brunelleschi's question as to how they were getting along with the information that, taking one consideration with another, they were getting along well in some areas, but badly in others.

'We're on the run,' he said. 'And we want to shelter here, Madame.'

'Who—who is running you?' asked she in great alarm. 'Not the police? If it is the police, mon cher, I have to ask you to leave immédiatement. The police I cannot risk to come to La Ronde.'

'Not the police,' said Levy. 'The police may indeed be after us, but not to our knowledge. No—the guys who're after us are the guys who gunned down those bent coppers Gaspardo and Delon—whose corpses we kindly disposed of for you.'

Her heavily-kohled eyes widened with shocked astonishment.

'Are you telling me,' she asked, 'that you know who it was who shot those two canaille?'

'Sure. And now they're after us.'

'You can prove this—that they fired the shots?'

'We can't—but any police ballistics expert could, simply by checking out their artillery.'

A massive weight seemed to fall from the stalwart shoulders of the redoubtable Mme Brunelleschi. Eyes flashing, she called out to the girls to 'fetch ma chère Nikki', contingent upon which there presently descended in the

glass and gilding lift a paunchy, small figure clad in a
spotted dress, a coarse apron, and a mob cap. The apparition
sported an enormous cigar in its wide and froglike mouth,
and, upon espying Levy and Fosdyke through black horn-
rimmed spectacles of excessive thickness, produced from its
person a revolver, which it pointed in their general direction
—and was only dissuaded from pulling the trigger by Mme
Brunelleschi interposing her considerable form between
shooter and target.

'Desist, chère Nikki!' cried Madame. These gentlemens
hold the key to your salvation. They know who rubbed out
Gaspardo and Delon, and can advise the police how to prove
it.'

Nikki—who turned out to be a woman of a forceful
personality, and, despite her lack of inches, plentitude of
girth and advancement of years, a formidable figure to
behold—put down her gun and grinned broadly at the two
men so described.

'Put it there, boys,' she grated in a deep corncrake of a
voice, and advanced a heavily-beringed hand for them both
to shake. 'You must be the fellers whom Madame was telling
me about—who carted away those two rats.'

Introductions effected, champagne was produced, and
Madame having declared that painting and decorating was
over for the day, the girls divested themselves of their coarse
aprons, in consequence of which they were much improved
in appearance.

'Is there a garage where we can park the car while we're
here?' asked Levy. 'It is kind of conspicuous outside.'

Mme Brunelleschi declared that this was no problem, for
there was a lock-up garage attached to the establishment
out the back. Accordingly, bartender Jules gave Fosdyke
and Levy a hand with the *Virgin*, whom they deposited, still
draped in canvas, in Madame's office; Levy then gave him
the keys to drive the Rolls to concealment.

'We will now have a party!' declared the genial proprietress of La Ronde, 'since the shadow of Madame Guillotine has been lifted from the shoulders of chère Nikki.'

Toasts were drunk to the latter, who then fell into conversation with Fosdyke and Levy. Though by appearance and accent a Parisian matron of the classic sort, the gang boss affected the vocal mannerisms of Messrs Edward G. Robinson, George Raft, Paul Muni and other thespians of the silver screen whose portrayal of gangsters so increased the gaiety of nations.

She inveighed with a seemingly first-hand bitterness against the Parisian police, with particular attention to Commissaire Orlando Sanson.

'If Madame hadn't sheltered me,' she said, 'that bastard Sanson and his side-kick Duval would have pulled me in, and, brother, little Nikki would have had the Third Degree. Innocence? I am here to tell you guys that innocence is a concept unknown among those dicks. I could have brought in my sainted mother to swear me a cast-iron alibi, likewise my parish priest, a member of the Chamber of Deputies who owes me not a few favours, half a dozen innocent children, and other witnesses of disinterested probity. They would have framed me and hung those cop-killings on to me just the same—totally innocent though I am.'

'Which reminds me that you owe me five thousand francs, Nikki,' said Mme Brunelleschi.

Nikki looked cunning—not a difficult feat. 'On account of what?' she inquired.

'That was what I paid you to rid me of Gaspardo and Delon,' replied the proprietress of La Ronde. 'Five thousand was your price. I paid you in cash. It doesn't matter that the acquaintances of these gentlemens here beat you to it.'

'It matters to *me*,' retorted Nikki Lamartine with some heat. 'I have my professional reputation to consider. What sort of credibility am I going to retain in the district if it gets around that I have allowed one of my clients the refund of a payment in advance on account of a mere technicality?'

Mme Brunelleschi grudgingly allowed Nikki Lamartine her point of technicality, and the party was resumed with no loss of good will.

Fosdyke, who had imbibed much Scotch and champagne in the course of a long evening, was looking askance at Yvonne, who was showing every sign of not suffering a lonely pillow that night. Mindful of his former success with the History of Cricket, he was considering a similar ruse when the girl Solange got up on a table and in a small, clear voice sang *Au Clair de la Lune*, and the fact that she was almost entirely nude in no way detracted from the simple innocence of her delivery. Mme Brunelleschi next obliged with a spirited rendition of *Le Rêve passe*, followed by *Le Chant de Départ* and *Ça Ira*—all good military-cum-revolutionary stuff. Levy then rose unsteadily to his feet and gave out with *The Whiffenpoof Song*, which constrained Fosdyke to attempt *The Eton Boating Song*, but he suffered a slight collapse in the second verse and fell asleep on the sofa.

When he woke up—alone and virginal—the wintry morning sun was filtering in through the cracks of the window shutters.

CHAPTER 11

The wife-and-mother-in-law slayer, having been questioned by the Examining Magistrate, Maître Delfont, and having cheerfully confessed to his fault in the pious hope (alas fruitless!) that the admission, coupled with a plea of a crime of passion, would save him from the guillotine, was committed to trial by jury. Commissaire Orlando Sanson, who had spent the morning kicking his heels outside the chambers, was then summoned by Maître Delfont and questioned about his progress in the killings of Gaspardo and Delon. Sanson, who, apart from ordering a search of the area that had opened up so many cans of worms, and also giving the order for the city and provinces to be scoured for the missing gang boss Nikki Lamartine, was put in the position of being obliged to extemporize.

'But, surely, Commissaire, you have some leads—something unusual must have been reported that night? Scarcely a night passes in Paris but some intelligent young officer notes down an occurrence that is out of the ordinary.'

Sanson puzzled his mind, and came out with a half-remembered gobbet of useless information that might satisfy the boringly persistent examining magistrate:

'There was one small point, monsieur,' he said. 'One of my fellows reported having seen a silver Rolls-Royce parked outside a brothel in the area. He didn't think anything of it at the time—didn't even trouble to take the number—but it came back to him after the murders were discovered.'

'You are seeking out this silver Rolls-Royce, of course?'

'Of course,' lied Sanson.

'It should not pose too much difficulty, Commissaire. There cannot be many such vehicles in Paris. Good day to you.'

Sanson walked out into the wintry sunshine, pulling his coat collar against the wind and thinking sourly of his wasted morning. Instead of going straight back to his office, he crossed over to a street-corner tabac that he occasionally favoured. It was kept by a widow named Juliette Pépin, a woman of good figure and bearing, but with the most villainous cross eyes.

'Good day, Commissaire,' she greeted him.

'Good day, Madame.' He picked up a pack of Gauloises.

'Would you care for a coffee? I'm just making.'

'That would be very agreeable. Thanks, Madame.'

She put up the 'Closed' sign and shut the door, then led the way into the small back room. A kettle was beginning to sing on a gas ring. Madame Pépin took off her apron and shook out her hair.

'Busy?' she asked.

He shrugged.

'It's nice to see you again. Won't you sit down?'

He took a seat on a large sofa that fairly filled the narrow room.

'You're a bit quiet today,' she said. 'I can tell you've got problems. Right?'

'Maybe,' he admitted.

She was on her knees before him and struggling with the laces of his brown and white-toned shoes. 'Can't you lend a hand?' she complained. 'Do I always have to undress you like a baby?'

Later, over the loom of light that shone through the window and the arc of her mouse-brown hair that was spread over his bare shoulder, he speculated upon the silver Rolls-Royce, and decided that—yes—it might be a good idea to follow it up. As that pompous ass Delfont had pointed out, there couldn't be all that many in Paris.

Levy spent most of the morning lingering by the telephone, ringing Oswald Zec's number every half-hour and receiving no reply. Towards noon, the two conspirators took counsel together and decided to leave it till nightfall and then quit Paris, find a hideout for themselves and the painting in the countryside, and make independent contact with Croesus with a view to setting up the sale and transfer without the aid of Zec as referee and middle-man. The only snag, as Levy was quick to point out, was that Croesus might take some convincing that they had indeed carried out the switch, and that the *Virgin* in their possession was the genuine item.

It was nearing midday, and they had joined Mme Brunel-leschi and Nikki in a magnum of champagne spiked with cognac when there came a peremptory knock on the street door.

'Tell them we're closed, Loulou,' said Madame, pouring more champagne into half-empty glasses.

Loulou went to the Judas window and, having made the brief announcement, was answered by a stentorian voice from beyond. The burden of the unseen visitor's argument was predicated by the one word 'Police'.

Madame was moved to instant action. Scarcely had Loulou shut the Judas window and turned his frightened face to her for guidance, than the enterprising proprietress issued her orders:

'Yvonne—conduct Nikki and these two gentlemens to the cellars. Jules—see to it that a large wine cask is rolled to cover over the cellar trapdoor after you have locked it. Go now—go, mes enfants. Leave everything to me!' A pause, as those concerned raced to do her bidding—and then: 'Admit the gentlemens of the law, Loulou.'

They came in. One glance was enough to tell the experienced proprietress of La Ronde that they were cut out of similar bolts of cloth as the two lately departed and largely unlamented Gaspardo and Delon. For a start, they were marginally too well-dressed for humble plain clothes men; their manner and bearing hardly differed in any respect from the small-time crooks and racketeers of the district who were supposed to be their natural prey. And they both smiled too much.

'Madame Brunelleschi?' inquired their spokesman—a big individual with washed-out blue eyes and a toothbrush moustache.

'Yes,' replied Madame. 'Can I help you?'

'I think so,' said the other. 'Officer Nattier and Officer Perchon.' He gave a perfunctory flash of a badge. 'Want to ask you a few questions.'

'First, would you care for a drink?'

'Not right now, Madame. Later, maybe. First, the questions. One: the other night—Tuesday, it was—a silver Rolls-Royce was reported outside your door. Whose was it?'

'I don't know, Officer. I have many clients. That night was—particularly busy.'

'Particularly busy.' He smiled at his companion, who smiled back. 'Mind if we take a look around?'

Madame bit her lip and said nothing, not even when they brushed past her and headed towards her office, which was marked: '*Privée*'; notwithstanding which, blue-eyed Nattier threw open the door and went in with Perchon at his heels.

It was Perchon who 'looked around'. He began by over-turning Madame's In-tray on to the desk and riffling care-lessly through the pile of invoices, receipts, letters, et cetera. While he was doing this, his colleague stood watching Mme Brunelleschi sidelong, a smile on his mean lips, gauging her reactions: her reactions were totally negative; she looked on impassively.

'I believe you used to do business with Inspector Gaspardo and Officer Delon,' said Nattier.

'I knew them both, certainly,' replied Madame.

'Better than that—you did business,' persisted Nattier.

'I don't know what you mean,' she replied.

The cut across her mouth with the back of his hand drew blood, but she did not cry out; merely took from her sleeve a lace handkerchief and dabbed her lips, throwing the detective a look of indescribable loathing and contempt as she did so.

'In future, for your information,' said Nattier, 'you do business with us—and you know what I mean. *Right?*'

'I know what you mean,' she replied.

'That's fine. Now you're talking sense. Over that drink you offered, we'll discuss terms—which will be weekly and in advance.'

It was then that Officer Perchon, who was continuing his looking around, came upon the large draped rectangle set against the far wall. He drew aside the canvas cover and gave a whistle.

'Pheeew! Look at this, Nattier!' he exclaimed.

The former turned and stared straight into the face of the *Virgin*.

'That's a hell of a picture to find in a brothel!' he declared. 'It's—familiar, too. Where have I seen it before?'

They had left the office door slightly ajar. It was kicked open the rest of the way. On the threshold stood a man in a thick trenchcoat and a slouch hat pulled low, but not so low that they could not see his face, which was that of a youngish man. He, like the two lawmen, smiled a lot; but it was not a sneering smile—more the wide-toothed grin of a bad boy enjoying his misbehaviour.

The silenced pistol in his hand coughed twice, and then again.

Nattier and Perchon fell where they stood, and without uttering a word or a cry.

Fosdyke and Levy, along with Nikki Lamartine, had sat around in the dark cellar all this time. Presently they heard the rumbling sound of the wine cask being rolled aside. The trapdoor was raised. Mme Brunelleschi peered down.

'Mr Levy,' she called.

'Yes?' answered he.

'There's a man to see you. Says he's a friend of yours. Will you come on up, he says, and bring your companion?'

Levy and Fosdyke exchanged glances. 'Could be Zec, though how in the hell he found us here has me beat,' said the former. 'So let's go.'

They climbed out of the cellar, Nikki following. It was the sudden shift from darkness to light, and the fact that the man in the hat and trenchcoat was standing with his back to a lacy-curtained window that delayed the moment of recognition.

The newcomer chuckled. 'Hi, Hal!' he said. 'Long time no see. Don't you remember your old buddy, hey?'

'Nat Willis!' exclaimed Levy. 'As I live and breathe— *Nat Willis!*'

Fosdyke felt, quite distinctly, a freezing finger trail down the length of his spine, and his whole skin crawled.

'I guess you had me lying at the bottom of the Atlantic, Hal,' said the newcomer. 'But it wasn't that way at all.'

'Then—*why? How?*' demanded Levy.

'Let's have ourselves a drink, Hal,' said Willis. 'And I'll tell you all about it.'

He stood aside and let them lead the way to the main reception room and the bar. And it was to be noticed by all that he held a silenced pistol in his right hand. Held loosely down by his side. But held, nevertheless.

He laid the pistol on the bar in front of him when he sat down. Levy and Fosdyke sat on his left—a little apart from him. He fixed it so.

'Hell, I thought you must be Oswald Zec,' declared Levy, by way of an opener.

Willis flashed his wild, bad-boy grin. 'Oswald met up with a slight accident,' he said, 'and won't be seen around —in a permanent kind of way.' He raised his Scotch. 'Your health, old comrade—and that of your talented new accomplice. I have to say in parentheses that I admire your switch, Mr Fosdyke. Couldn't have figured a better one myself. It had class.'

'Your switch of the *Mona Lisa* was a classic, also, Nat,' said Levy. 'See how it's stood the test of time.' He took a deep swallow of his drink. 'You were going to tell all about it, Nat,' he added quietly.

Again the zany grin. 'Hal, you know me for what I am —or what I was till we met up in that café. I'm a loner, Hal. A born loner. Oh, it was great working with you on the *Mona Lisa* switch. But I got restless.' He chuckled. 'And I also got greedy.'

'You ran out on me, sure,' said Levy. 'But you weren't so greedy as to forget to leave me my cut of the proceeds in the ship's safe.'

Willis shook his head, still grinning. 'I left you exactly one quarter of the take, Hal,' he said. 'And that for old time's sake, merely. I like you, pal. But I grew so I wanted to work alone again. So I staged my falling overboard, and had a crewman smuggle me ashore at Le Havre. Pity about that guy: he had a nasty accident—drowned in the tideway of the Seine. So helpful, too.' He chuckled.

'Let me get this straight, Nat,' said Levy. 'You say that you left me only a quarter of the take—but Croesus paid out only fifty thousand bucks—and you left me my whole twenty-five share.'

Willis shook his head and winked. 'Croesus paid out twice that amount, Hal,' he said. 'With a little help from Zec— who was only too willing to pick up his boss's payment for helping out with the deal, and also to taking a cut from me —I put the squeeze on the Big Guy and made him pay out double. It was either that, I said, or I'd blow the whole deal to the papers.

'After my untimely "death", I went south to Monte Carlo, where I've been doing very nicely, thank you. Nothing very big—not like your new Leonardo switch—but with no one to split the proceeds with but myself.'

'And then,' said Levy, 'along came *The Virgin of the Rocks*.'

The other chuckled. 'Like you said, along she came,' he assented. 'I had it from Zec, who kept in touch with me. From there on in, I had the latest on all your doings, just as you reported them to Zec and Croesus.' He gazed long and hard at his former accomplice. 'I'm going to have that picture, Hal,' he added. 'And I'm fresh out of charity for old time's sake. There'll be no cut for you—nor for friend Fosdyke.'

'I get the message, Nat,' said Levy.

'So do I,' added Fosdyke, who had been listening to the exchange with a grim premonition of the outcome. 'So how about another drink?'

'I like your new accomplice, Hal,' grinned Willis. 'Like I said, he's got style.'

'You both have style, Nat,' replied Levy. 'That's why I

chose you.' He picked up the glass that Jules the bartender had just recharged. 'Here's to us—and the *Virgin*.'

There had been no furtive communion between Fosdyke and Levy, no nods and winks, no kicks or nudges; but the moment Willis next raised his glass, they both moved as one. On their feet and lunging, both.

They both stopped, checked in mid-pace, as the unwavering muzzle of the silenced pistol was presented to both of them, one by one.

'Sit down again and take it easy, fellers,' grinned Willis. 'All I want is the *Virgin*, and no one else gets hurt—especially my old buddy and his new side-kick.

'Speaking of virgins—' he glanced across to where, at the far angle of the bar, Mme Brunelleschi sat flanked by Nikki Lamartine and the faithful Yvonne; the rest of the girls had fled to their rooms, and Loulou also. 'Come over here and have a drink with me and my pals, ladies,' he said.

They came. Whatever Yvonne's private thoughts—and possible fears—about the killer, she was all professional: full of brittle smiles and endearments, her hand resting lightly on Willis's shoulder, while he imprisoned her slender and not over-encumbered waist with one arm. The pistol lay close to his other hand.

'I like you, babe,' he confided, grinning widely.

'You wanna go upstairs with me, big boy?' she purred.

'It's on the house,' interposed Madame. 'Just to celebrate that we won't be having any further trouble.'

'That's mighty generous of you, ma'am,' declared Willis. He drained his glass and grinned at Levy. 'Hal, old buddy, the time has come for the parting of the ways. Begging your leave, but I'm going to lock you and Mr Fosdyke back in the cellar till after I've gone, when I shall hand Madame the key. It's goodbye, Hal.'

He held out his hand—and Levy took it.

*

They sat side by side in the darkness. Presently Levy said: 'Now you've seen what a real criminal mentality is like in action, Bernie. He must have wiped out Zec, like you and I would poison a rat—just because he happens to be in the way. A nuisance. A complication who insists on sharing our crust.'

'He's spared us,' said Fosdyke, 'so he can't be all bad.'

'Sentiment,' said Levy. 'At last, as regards me. As far as you're concerned, his professionalism respects your style. That's Nat Willis all over. Can always be relied upon to do the unexpected. The quixotic. The off-beat.'

'What now?' asked Fosdyke. 'I take it we can kiss goodbye to the *Virgin*?'

'As good as,' said the other. 'Of course, we can blow the whole thing sky-high by sending the story to the papers, but we won't do that. And Nat Willis knows we won't do that —if only for the reason that it would ruin the life of that poor sucker de Courcey. Pity of it is, that if you want to find that girl of yours again, you'll have to do it on your own flat feet. No money to buy yourself half the private eyes in Paris to search her out. Why in the hell did you two have a fight, anyhow? You only met a couple of times. Why did you let her go? Tell me.'

So Fosdyke told him—everything. And when he had done, Levy clucked his tongue and shook his head in the darkness.

'All that—because you saw her get into a flash car with some guy!'

'*Two* guys—*different* guys. And *two* flash cars.'

'And on that slender premise, you have her written in as a scarlet woman! This is a simple case of basic sexual jealousy, and you are making of it a three-act tragic opera. I will remind you of the crack from *Othello*, by William Shakespeare. It is Iago who speaks:

> *Trifles light as air*
> *Are to the jealous confirmations strong*
> *As proofs of holy writ.*"

'That's you. You are all snarled up with sexual jealousy of no very sound provenance.'

They were both silent for a while, and then Fosdyke said: 'You're right, Hal. At least, I think you are. You usually are. So, as soon as possible, I'm going to start searching for her. No matter how long it takes me, I'll find her. And then I'm going to ask her to marry me—before she has time to hop into another flash car with another guy!'

Along with the darkness, the silence closed in on them again.

The note of their freedom from the cellar was a high note, jollity held lightly in check the leitmotif.

'You can come out now,' declared Madame. 'He's gone!'

With her was Yvonne, still in her working wrapper. And the other girls crowded around—all smiling. Nikki Lamartine also.

'What happened?' asked Levy. 'You all look like you've come into a legacy.'

'Come and see—come and see!' They seized the two by the hands—Yvonne and Madame, Solange and Marie, even Nikki Lamartine—and half-pulled, half-coaxed them out into the main reception room and towards Madame's office.

'Close your eyes!'

'Surprise, surprise!'

Eyes closed, they were led into the office, hands still gently imprisoned.

'Eyes open now!'

And they were standing by the wall and staring across the room to the fireplace, above which hung the picture, their picture, Leonardo's picture of the Virgin and her companions. In that ill-furnished, badly-lit room, they stood out in glory and gilded their surroundings with splendour, shouting for joy.

'But—how? *How?*'

'Well, we guessed that it was the picture he sought,' said Madame. 'It was Nikki who had the big idea, and gave it to us. While he was upstairs with Yvonne, we fixed things. When he came down, he made Loulou and Jules load what he had come here for into his pantechnicon waiting outside. And he drove off, rejoicing.'

'But—*with what?*' cried Fosdyke.

'With a coffee table underneath the canvas cover,' said Madame. 'In the upstairs lounge there was a coffee table almost exactly the same size as the painting. We knocked off its legs, wrapped it in the canvas and hid the painting. And he never suspected. Never guessed. Not for one instant.'

A council of war followed.

'He'll be back,' declared Levy, who knew their opponent —none better. 'As soon as he discovers the switch, he'll be right back in here again, just like he was before.'

'Not so easily,' interposed Nikki Lamartine. 'I checked out that he forced the one and only back window on the ground floor. Right now, Jules is boarding it up and resting a wine cask against it. Does this guy have any team to back him up?'

Levy shook his head. 'He's a loner.'

Nikki lit a fat cigar. 'Then, if he shows, he's as good as croaked,' she drawled. 'I can call upon fifty guys at a moment's notice, a hundred in an hour. They will surround this place and render it like it was a fortress. The cops I cannot keep out. Any single two-bit heister, it's a stroll. But there are a couple things I can't handle. These you guys will have to fix.'

'Say it,' said Levy.

'One: you must dispose of those two dead cops,' said Nikki. 'This for Madame's peace of mind. Two: you will win my eternal gratitude if you could only direct the mind of M. le Commissaire towards the idea that someone else, and not yours sincerely, croaked Gaspardo and Delon.'

'I think that can be done,' replied Levy. He met Fosdyke's astonished eye. 'In fact, I have already got me a couple of ideas running around in my head that could kill these two particular birds you mention with one stone.'

Fosdyke shrugged. It was clearly his partner's night for ideas. He himself was too tired, bemused and boozed to think straight.

CHAPTER 12

Early morning in the Place de la Concorde, with the whiff of newly-roasted coffee in the air, and the streets slippery with fresh snow re-frozen in the chill dawn. And nobody venturing out; most particularly thankfully, no policemen—as Levy brought the silver Rolls to a gliding halt as near to the plate-glass front doors of the Hotel Crillon as he was able.

They both got out and walked quickly away, towards the telephone booth situated at the other side of the entrance to the Rue Royale. (Fosdyke stole a wistful glance up the latter street, towards the café where he had first sat with Dorothy Batthyány—and would surely sit again, if the golden-faced beings who live up on Mount Olympus and direct our fates upon their whim would only smile upon him.)

They piled into the booth together, grateful for their mutual warming. Levy made the call . . .

'Quai des Orfèvres? Listen, for I'm not repeating this. Write it down. Don't try to be smart—just listen. Police Officers Nattier and Perchon have been murdered. That's what I said—murdered. Shot. Their bodies are in the boot of a silver Rolls-Royce which is parked at this moment outside the Hotel Crillon. Got that? No—you're crazy if you think I'm going to wait around till the squad cars arrive.'

He rang off, winked at his companion, and dialled another number.

'Crillon? Connect me with Room 210, please.

'Hello, there. This is Henry Higgins. Yes—Higgins. Listen, the merchandise is lying in the boot of my silver Rolls-Royce which is right outside the front door of your hotel at this very moment. The car door's open and the key's in the ignition. I suggest you dispose of both car and picture in a safe hiding place before the police start asking questions. Where am I right now? That's my business. Don't worry, I'll be in touch, and we'll discuss terms then. Good luck to you. Oh—and—Heil Hitler!'

He replaced the earpiece and grinned at his companion, who grinned back.

'I suggest we stay right here,' said Fosdyke.

'Excellent idea,' responded Levy. 'Here we have a grandstand view of the whole proceedings. Snug and warm, with every convenience save popcorn, ice-cream, candy, and soda-pop.'

The Herr Rittmeister, pausing only to throw on his greatcoat over his pyjamas and smoking jacket (badges, decorations and all), step into a pair of half-boots and clap his hat on the side of his shaven head (the monocle was still firmly in place), burst out into the lobby of his de luxe suite, where his two henchmen were slumped, asleep and fully-dressed, in armchairs; they had been scouring the streets in the ten blocks adjacent to the accommodation lately used by Levy and Fosdyke, and had abandoned the search only an hour previously.

'On your feet, idle swinehounds!' snarled the autocrat. 'Load your pistols and follow me!' And he tore out of the suite and, scorning to wait for the elevator, leapt down the stairs with the verve and dash of a ski champion—which he had lately been.

The Herr Rittmeister was first at the Rolls by a considerable lead, and was struggling to open the boot when his panting minions joined him.

'I think it is locked, Herr Rittmeister,' suggested Moustache and Glasses.

'Dolt! Imbecile! Blockhead! That solution had not escaped my notice!' blazed the autocrat. 'Get into the car, both of you! We will drive to a garage and have the boot forced open!'

The key, as had been promised, was in the ignition. The monocled ex-officer took his place in the driving seat and switched on. A touch of the starter button and the great engine purred silkily to life. He depressed the clutch pedal and snicked off the handbrake.

And then the line of police patrol cars tore into the great square, two-toned sirens blaring; circled the monolithic obelisk set upon its island in the centre, and turned in towards the Hotel Crillon, where their sighted quarry was just moving off to cut across their front and head away up the Champs Elysées. The lead patrol car immediately turned to give chase.

The hunt was up!

From their warm vantage point in the telephone booth, the two watchers hugged each other in delight.

Now he was no longer driving a silver Rolls-Royce up the Champs Elysées; instead, the Herr Rittmeister, Order of Pour le Mérite, Iron Cross, First and Second Class, was fleeing before impossible odds, his Fokker DVII riddled from prop to rudder, his guns silent and out of ammunition, and the faltering engine sucking in the last few litres of precious gasoline.

On his tail, a line of Sopwith Camels, who had murderously dived upon the lone Fokker from out of a cloud, had ripped it with lead and were now hell-bent upon destroying man and machine before they could reach the safety of the German lines.

To his left, Le Café de la Paix—that surely marked the English forward base at Bertincourt. The lines lay only five kilometres on. He was still climbing up the Champs Elysées. The Arc de Triomphe was dead ahead; he tensed his fingers on the joystick, ready to pull back and soar over the top of the great archway. That was the beauty of the DVII—it could outclimb any Camel. The men in the back were screaming with fear. He had no recollection of having brought passengers with him; there was no room in a DVII for passengers.

'Herr Rittmeister—for pity's sake slow down!'

One of the Camels—the leader—was making to come alongside him. A sharp, cutting-out sideslip, and the enemy pilot thought better of it; dropped back.

The great arch represented the German lines. Once over No-Man's Land, he could begin to make his descent. He would dive with engine opened right out. The sturdy Fokker would survive the massive strains upon its structure; if the Camels dared to do likewise, they would strip their wings.

As the lines drew close, he tensed his hands to pull back the joystick and soar over the top of the arch. Nothing happened!

'Herr Rittmeister—turn right! Heaven—you'll kill us all!'

He ploughed on—straight through the archway and out the other side. And the Camels now came at him from both left and right, they having turned both ways to circumvent the soaring monolith of marble.

Ahead was the descent. Shouting a wild pæan of victory into the slipstream, he opened up the throttle and tore down the slope of the Avenue de la Grande Armée at maximum revolutions.

A wild-eyed glance back over his shoulder, and he rejoiced to see that the Camels were dropping back. Ahead, and slightly to the left, the dark smudge of the Bois de Boulogne marked the woods surrounding his goal: the forward aerodrome of the famous 'Flying Circus', of which, along with old Hermann, Ernst, Erich, Lothar and the rest of Jagdgeschwäder 1, he was an outstanding ace in the Imperial Flying Corps, with thirty victories painted in Allied roundels on the side of the Fokker's fuselage.

Almost home. Tonight, they would dine off the mess silver, and he would offer the champagne . . .

What was that?

'*Herr Rittmeister!—More police cars! Aaaaa!—Look out!*'

They were coming from left and right, dead ahead, making to block his passage with their fuselages. Not Camels this time. More like Spad 13s. Americans or French. Well, he would fly right through them—and take a couple of them with him if he had to!

The hurtling Rolls missed hitting two police cars drawn across its path by a skin of paint, left and right. Once through, the silvery projectile went into an uncontrolled and uncontrollable front-wheel skid and ended up against the bole of a substantial chestnut tree. The car was only superficially damaged, for the bridge-like construction of the chassis was proof against the most devastating crash; not so the three occupants, whose tender frames were not designed to absorb the effects of instant deceleration from eighty miles an hour to zero; nor had they been belted into the phantom Fokker DVII.

Around midday, Levy opted to go back to La Ronde and report on their morning's work; he also wanted to make sure, he said, that Willis had not returned and by some miracle spirited the *Virgin* from its hiding-place behind a massive array of wine casks and racks in the locked cellar. He had a shrewd idea that Fosdyke would opt to remain in and around the Rue Royale district: it was a correct appreciation.

Fosdyke pretended to himself that there were things he had to seek out and buy: a new razor (though his old one, which had seen much service, was still perfectly usable), a handkerchief or two, a pair of socks, a hairbrush. All these he purchased with one eye on the clock, and a profound inner conviction that time must have stood still, or at least was only moving at half speed. At a quarter to the hour—*their* hour—he had done all his shopping and was adrift at the end of the Rue Royale with a carrier bag full of purchases, fifteen minutes to kill, and nowhere to go. And the last place on earth he wanted to be seen was in *their* café before the hour struck.

It was hopeless, of course. And his natural diffidence was no help. He should stride right into that café, beard the friendly waiter and demand to know if Dorothy had been in since the last time. The answer would almost certainly be no—but a start would be made. After that, he would scour the whole of Paris (no, not the whole of Paris, Dorothy had said she lived 'not far from here'), and now that they had recovered possession of the *Virgin* (but had probably lost touch with the buyer), the prospect of being able to spend a lot of money on professional assistance greatly enhanced his hopes of locating her.

He mulled all this over for a while, and was then surprised to see that time had flown and that it was five minutes past the hour. He ran the last fifty yards to the café.

He took a seat at the 'usual' table.

'Monsieur désire?—Aaaaah!—Bonjour, m'sieu.'

It was friendly Jean. He did not need to be told what the score was, for Fosdyke's anxious, questioning expression was informative enough. And he had some of the answers.

'Madame 'as been back every day,' he vouchsafed.

'Oh no!' exclaimed Fosdyke, delighted beyond belief.

'And the last day when it was you came,' continued the other, 'she was 'ere only a minute after you 'ad gone. So I say to hair: "M'sieu, 'e 'as just gone." So she look very disappoint—and she is back every day. Why—'ere she his!'

Dorothy was wearing a long woollen coat, a long scarf, a

woollen beret with a pom-pom on the top. Her eyes were alight, and surely must be matching his.

'Hello, Bernard,' she said.

'Hello, Dorothy.'

'Mind if I sit down?'

'Of course.' He pulled out a chair for her, eased it forward as she seated herself. At close quarters, he could smell her scent, which reminded him of summer days on a pine-crested hillside.

Jean brought a vase containing four perfect daffodils, and gave Fosdyke an anxious, quizzical glance.

'How's the book?' she asked, when they were facing each other again. 'Has your publisher made an offer?'

'Not yet.'

'It must be very frustrating, the waiting.'

'It is, rather.'

'Bernard, I . . .'

'Dorothy, I . . .'

'Sorry.'

'No, it's all right, Bernard. You first.'

'I was going to say that I saw you the other day. You were in a Mercedes with a man—an older man. I followed after, but lost you.'

'Oh, what a pity. I was with Beppo, and he'd have loved to meet you.'

'Beppo?'

'My father—stepfather, actually. He's a dear.'

'But—I saw you another time—the day we met—and you were getting into another car, with another chap.'

'Ah, that would have been by arrangement.'

'By—arrangement?'

'That was Frédéric—Beppo's chauffeur. When I'm out shopping and things around the faubourg, he often cruises around, picks me up and takes me home.'

He looked at her sidelong: doubtful, dismayed. 'You live in very grand style,' he said.

'Yes, I suppose we do, really. I never think about it.'

'You told me you lived in squalor.'

'It is *pretty* squalid. The plumbing in those pre-French Revolution mansions in the faubourg has to be seen to be believed. No self-respecting American would be seen dead in any one of our seven bathrooms.'

'You told me,' he said, 'that you shared with six other people.'

She laughed. 'That was very teasing of me, but it's quite true. There's Beppo, me—and five servants living in.'

'Oh—I see.'

Dorothy looked at him askance for a few moments, then her eyes brightened, and something suspiciously like a blush suffused her smooth cheeks.

'Bernard, tell me . . .'

'What?'

'Well, when you were grumpy and offhand with me last time, I thought it was because you'd decided that you didn't like me as much as you thought you might. But—it wasn't like that at all, was it?'

'No,' he admitted.

'It was—about Frédéric, wasn't it? And, afterwards, I suppose, about Beppo?'

He nodded, and avoided her eyes. 'Something like that.'

Her glance was quite unwavering. 'So, you were grumpy and offhand with me, not because you were disappointed in me—which was why I was so upset and humiliated that I ran away—but because you were jealous. Is that right, Bernard?'

He met her gaze, and rejoiced in what he saw there. 'Yes, that was it, Dorothy,' he admitted.

Their hands met across the table, and Fosdyke's heart leapt. This adorable, outspoken girl, this beautiful and suddenly available creature of perfection would be his. There might be mountains to climb and rivers to be bridged. Beppo, the mansion in the faubourg, the fleet of cars, the squad of living-in servants—they constituted a circle that would have to be squared somehow.

But—as man and woman—there was no impediment between them. Not any longer.

At about that time, Nathan T. Willis—who had hard-driven his pantechnicon through the night with only a short break at a wayside pull-in for a cup of coffee and a half-hour snooze —drove through Vienne and climbed the dry, sage-covered hills where the cicadas shrilled and twittered under the fitful, wintry sunlight. Before him, the road south ran straight beside the swollen river on its way to the Mediterranean.

Over the next rise, he was looking down into a valley, where a railway line crossed the road. There was a gated level-crossing, a clapboard hut with smoke rising from its chimney, a tired horse with a sagging back tethered to a rail fence. And a dog barked.

The pantechnicon had had a hard night of it—as had he —and he let it cruise down the steep hill with no foot on the accelerator, and thought that maybe he would stop off at the next town and have a shave and a brush-up, followed by a steak and a half-bottle of wine. The thought revived his tired senses.

Approaching the level-crossing, he saw an old man come out of the hut and stroll, in no great hurry, towards the gates; the fellow was about to begin closing them when he noticed the pantechnicon coming down the road towards him. At this, he looked right, then at his watch, following upon which he gave a shrug, leaned against the gate and waved Willis to come on. Which Willis did.

The railway track was laid upon a raised hump of shingle, and when the pantechnicon's front wheels bit upon the yielding mass, they began to slip. Willis, blaming himself that he had not taken the slight gradient at a smarter speed, gunned the engine a couple of times, missed his footing on the pedal, and cursed when the thing coughed and died. Right in the middle of the track.

The old crossing-keeper came up to him and shouted through the window: 'Can't stop here. The train's due. Get her going, will you!'

Brushing aside this totally unnecessary annoyance, Willis pressed the starter button. The starter motor whirred. No ignition.

More exasperated than scared, more amused at the absurdity of the situation than exasperated, Willis persisted in his attempts to restart the engine; but half aware that his efforts were counter-productive and becoming increasingly so. He had flooded the carburettor. The drill with that particular engine was to leave it alone, smoke a cigarette, and then start again.

Only—he didn't have time to smoke a cigarette.

The old crossing-keeper was shouting now, and pointing away down the line. Willis broke into the other's wild warning that the driver of the oncoming train would never see the blocked track in time to pull up.

'All right, all right! Stop panicking, then, and give me a push!'

To give him his due, the old fellow turned to with a will, exerting all his puny strength against the rear of the vehicle, while Willis—since he had nothing to lose in so doing, and he might have been lucky—resumed his attempts to restart the engine. Nothing resulted from either of their efforts.

And then the old man gave up. With a wild cry, he took to his heels and ran to safety.

Willis was out of the driving seat with the shrill screech of the oncoming locomotive's whistle dinning in his ears. He wrenched open the rear door of the pantechnicon and, grabbing hold of the shrouded shape that lay across the folded-down rear seats of the big vehicle, dragged it towards him. This at least he would save—along with his own life ...

And then the efforts of his frantic fingers dislodged the canvas covering, and instead of looking down at the serene face of *The Virgin of the Rocks,* he was staring at the top of a coffee table: an old and careworn coffee table, ringed and stained and pock-marked with cigarette burns.

The wild bad-boy gave a bellowing laugh of self-mockery that was near to tears. He was still laughing when the locomotive struck him, full on.

The discovery of the bodies of the murdered police detectives Nattier and Perchon in the locked boot of the crashed Rolls-Royce, together with the guns belonging to the dead Germans—two of which were found to be those that had fired the bullets which earlier killed Gaspardo and Delon—had the Paris Police Department on its ear.

Even greater puzzlement awaited the Paris police, however—though the mills of God were grinding particularly slowly in this instance, and much time would elapse before evidence reached them that the pistol found upon the body of an unknown man who had been killed on a railway level-crossing south of Vienne was the very same that had slain Nattier and Perchon in the capital some twenty-four hours previously.

But on the purely parochial level, these revelations were for many months overshadowed by the shooting of Commissaire Orlando Sanson by his wife Mathilde, and by the apocryphal accounts of how she remained by his bedside, day and night, in the hospital of Saint-Louis, and he with tubes sticking out of every orifice in the attempt to quicken the flickering flame of his life; while long and loud the wretched woman begged her unconscious spouse to live, in return for which she promised faithfully—in her own reported words—to 'be a good wife and behave myself'.

Fosdyke saw little, during the busy weeks that followed, of his late partner in crime, for Levy declared himself to be 'involved', and hinted that he was making plans to travel on. They met, however, on a couple of occasions, and Fosdyke reported on his doings, in particular that he was now engaged to Dorothy Batthyány—with her stepfather's wholehearted support, furthermore.

Upon his prospective stepfather-in-law's insistence, he had moved into a suite of rooms in the seventeenth-century mansion in the Rue du Faubourg St Honoré which had once been the town house of one of Louis XV's farmers-general and had been Dorothy's Paris residence ever since her mother (now deceased) had married the multi-millionaire Austrian chain-store magnate Alfons ('Beppo') von Bruno. It was there, at the Hôtel de Martini, that he had a telephone call from Levy, asking him to join him for dinner that same evening at their favourite tête-de-veau restaurant, adding two items of information to sweeten the invitation: one, that he was 'moving on' tomorrow; two, that he had sold the *Virgin* for a good price.

Fosdyke was at the restaurant on time; Levy was already seated, wearing a tuxedo, with the inevitable carnation buttonhole. The two friends and fellow criminals shook hands.

'You're looking good, Hal,' said Fosdyke.

'You're looking not too bad yourself, Bernie,' replied Levy. 'Enough charm and looks to win a whole bevy of heiresses. But I'll never know how you managed to sell yourself to a guy like Beppo von Bruno, who, by all accounts, is reputed to be the hardest-headed businessman in central Europe.'

Fosdyke laughed. 'Beppo is a very sincere person,' he said. 'His great wish is to have Dorothy marry and be happy. Naturally, he didn't want her to marry a fortune-hunter, but he's bright enough to know that some of the most dedicated fortune-hunters are people who already have fortunes of their own. So he actively encouraged her to date every kind of suitor. This amused Dorothy—she called it "studying human nature".'

'And in the end, she fell for your brand of human nature
—and so did Beppo. I've got to hand it to you.' Levy poured
them both bumper glasses of the house red wine. 'You have
hidden depths.'

'Beppo made his fortune in chain stores,' said Fosdyke.
'All he ever wanted to be, however—and so he confided to
me—was a writer. He said: "Bernard, a writer need make
no more capital investment, take no more risk, than the cost
of an exercise book and a pencil, a typewriter at most."
When he found that I was a writer—and that I've just had
an offer for my first book—I couldn't put a foot wrong.'

Their tête-de-veau was brought by Madame, who had
sufficiently unbent, now that they were more or less 'regu-
lars', as to be all smiles. The two friends addressed themselves to their plates for quite a while.

Presently Fosdyke said: 'Great news that you've managed
to sell the *Virgin*, Hal.'

'Thought you'd never allude to the subject,' Levy said
wryly. 'I guess a cool half-million is peanuts to a guy who's
about to marry an heiress, but it's going to help me out no
end in my new enterprise—of which more later.'

'Who did you sell it to?' asked Fosdyke. 'Not Croesus, I
suppose?'

'No, no,' said Levy. 'Croesus put himself right out of the
running by letting Nat Willis double-cross me. Add to that,
he'd never have bought the unauthenticated picture. No, I
sold it to a guy who accepted an entirely new provenance I
put upon it.'

'Which was . . .?'

'That our *Virgin* is yet another version by Leonardo, and
that it had been stolen from a monastery in Perugia during
the mid-nineteenth century, a fact about which the prospective buyer should keep very dark or the Order of St Benedict
might commence a legal action for its recovery.'

'Brilliant, Hal. Really brilliant.'

'Well, your half-million I've deposited in a numbered

Swiss bank account, details of which are in here.' He laid an envelope by Fosdyke's wine glass. 'Me, I'm off to Soviet Russia tomorrow—in my new Rolls-Royce.'

'Russia, Hal? *Russia?* But what's there for *you?*'

'The Hermitage Museum, Leningrad, for a start. The finest picture gallery in the world, with the greatest collection of the art of all countries and periods gathered together under one roof. There, for a start, I hope to get my hands on a couple of prime Rembrandts—using the classic switches numbers one and two, devised by the late Nat Willis (and, by the way, I sent a wreath from our anonymous selves to his funeral in Vienne) and yourself respectively.'

After dinner they repaired to the Deux Magots, cradle of their late great triumph, and there decided to 'make a night of it'. Taking all in all, their farewell meeting was a joyful affair, well-laced at its close with the twin spirits of friendship and Scotland. They parted company outside the café, and Fosdyke watched his friend make his unsteady way up the Boulevard St-Germain till Levy had passed out of sight.

He never saw the big blond man again.

On a morning in the very early spring, so early that the first chestnut blossom in the Champs Elysées was no more than a budding promise, M. de Courcey, the retired Temporary Acting Director of the Louvre Museum, accompanied Mlle Lebrun in a chauffeur-driven Bugatti touring limousine on the road to the Loire. They had with them, for refreshment on the way, a hamper from Fauchon's comprising caviar, oyster patties in the English style, Bath Oliver biscuits plastered generously with pâté de foie gras, truffles in aspic, frogs' legs in a piquant sauce, slices of rare roast beef in pastry; together with imported Channel Island strawberries and Normandy cream, prodigious profiteroles, chocolate gâteau, and lime and chocolate sorbet. And a magnum of champagne on ice.

M. de Courcey wore a dove-grey morning suit, with a

flowered waistcoat, a black top hat, pale violet spats over patent leather pumps, dove-grey gloves and cravat. Across his slender stomach was swagged a gold half-hunter watch on a heavy gold chain—a present from Mlle Lebrun, who was in a costume by Molyneux: a silk two-piece in subtle tones of beige contrasted with black velvet braiding and topped by a mink coat worn dégagé over one shoulder, with a Cossack-style hat in the same skins. Her make-up was by Helena Rubinstein, her silk stockings by Markova, jewellery by Cartier.

They journeyed by way of Villers-sur-Orge, Angerville, Orléans, Beaugency (where they took their picnic lunch overlooking the River Loire), Blois, Tours and Vouvray.

In all that time, they scarcely exchanged a word; but, save for when they were enjoying luncheon, held hands all the way to the château.

The wedding of Dorothy Batthyány and Bernard Fosdyke was set for May 1st. Two weeks before that event, Beppo von Bruno gave them the key of his surprise wedding present: a handsome studio apartment in a most desirable part of Montparnasse. Accordingly, the happy couple drove out to Montparnasse to view their new town property (Dorothy already had a villa in Cap d'Ail which had belonged to her late mother, and a farmhouse near Aix-en-Provence which had been left to her by her paternal grandfather).

The apartment was on the mezzanine floor of a splendid new block that had been designed by a follower of Le Corbusier. It had its own private elevator and comprised four reception rooms, four bedrooms and the usual offices.

'This, darling, is your study,' said Dorothy, when they came to an L-shaped room whose picture window commanded a splendid view of the Montparnasse cemetery's baroque splendours. 'So incredibly gothic-romantic, the Castle of Fratta and all. How very bright of Beppo to be so attuned to your slightly macabre proclivities—and he hasn't even read your book yet.'

Fosdyke smiled with pleasure, and let his hand run over the yielding leather backrest of the captain's chair that faced the partners' desk that housed a built-in typewriter, recording machine, wireless set, and a cinematograph projector. And thought back to the mean bedsitting-room—it was during his encyclopædia days—where he had cobbled out, night by night, the pages of his first book.

The rest of the apartment was similarly a delight to the eye and the æsthetic and luxury-loving senses. Their bedroom was a stage-set from a romantic ballet by Petipa, the kitchen would have been quite at home at the functional end of the Tour d'Argent. The bathroom, with its sunken sea-shell of a plunge bath and the life-sized and gilded dolphin that forever spouted water (hot to cold at the touch of a lever), was pure Beverly Hills.

They came, at length, to the drawing-room. Like Fosdyke's study, this also was L-shaped, and presented, upon entry, a medley of the ancient and the modern. The principal furnishings were seventeenth-century Venetian, the carpets Chinese and Persian. A stunning Braque still life faced an Augustus John portrait of a ballerina in the short arm of the L, and the chandelier spoke of the Hall of Mirrors at Versailles.

'Beppo really has the most excellent taste,' observed Fosdyke.

'He chose it all himself,' said Dorothy. 'Wouldn't take any advice from anyone, he told me. What goes on round here? Oh! . . .' She paused at the angle of the L, looking down into the longer arm. Fosdyke, taking the two or three steps to join her, saw the glory written in her eyes, and had an immediate premonition.

The Virgin of the Rocks—their own, their very own *Virgin* —his and Levy's, and now Dorothy's also—was hung above a Renaissance chimneypiece, and looked as if it belonged there and had been there for ever.

'So *this* is what Beppo has been so not-too-secretive about,' said Dorothy. 'It's a copy, of course, but he made vague noises about it being the real thing—an undiscovered version by Leonardo's own hand, but not a word to anyone about *that*, my dear! It is rather splendid, though, isn't it, darling?' She put her hand in his and they both looked up at the face of the Madonna. 'I do so hope it won't be too grand for us.'

'Not at all,' said Fosdyke. 'She was made for us.'

Fosdyke had only one communication from Harold Hiram Levy: a card posted from Warsaw, dated Friday, March 17, 1933, on which he said he was waiting for his visa to enter the USSR and the booze and grub were fine.

But on the first anniversary of Switch Number Two, the attendants in the Florentine section of the Louvre picture galley were surprised to find a dark red carnation tucked into a corner of the frame surrounding *The Virgin of the Rocks*. And—except for 1941 to 1946—for very many years after on that same date.